MONEY IS KING

Nicety

Copyright © 2013 **Denise Entertainment**

Facebook: nicetycouture

Twitter: @NicetyCouture

Website: www.nicetyzone.com

YouTube: mswordpoison

Instagram: iamnicety

ACKNOWLEDGEMENTS

Giving honor to God; who is the head of my
household. Thank you to my family; I will love

you all until the end of time, you are the air that

I breathe.

To my friends; thanks for keeping me afloat

when I thought I would sink.

To my fans and many followers; I love you

all more than words can say.

Thank you for the love and support

you deliver each day!

DEDICATION

I would like to dedicate this book to my family and my friends
who supported my dream of becoming a published writer.
They believed in me when I didn't believe in myself years ago.
I'm making you proud now! Also to my readers for
without you there would be no me. I love you all!
To some very special readers who have been rocking
with me and supporting me from day one, I love you all.
This book goes out to my editor Latosha Scruggs,
Jackie Figueroa, Fallon Willis Blaqk, Keyanna Savage,
Shemika Jones, Sharon Blount, Courtney Bryant,
Keona Day, LaShaun Cadney, Rosalyn Reed, Shanta Shaw,
Me'Tova Hollingsworth, LaSonya Steger, Lakenya Ross,
Candice Preyer, Tiffany Williams, Nae Martinez, Shikira Hoy,
Tona McCoy, Shamella Skipper, Linda Jiggets,
Marissa Palmer, Sistar Tea, Sandy Sims, Carla Towns,
Brandie Davis, Joy Hammond Nelson and Tanisha-PhatPhat.
and last but certainly not least The Nicety Readers!!!
Love you all!
Special Shout outs to #TEAMNICETY, the bullets
to my nine!
To my besties...you all know who you are as I will only
use first names but your love and support knows no bounds.
Mario, Guillermo, Ashley H., Yvette, Bob, Manny
"You're so silly", Leslie, Princess, Walt, Will, Karen, Theresa,
Irine, Meron, Jermika and MY LATE AUNT-IN-LAW Earline.
I want to thank you from the bottom of my heart
for always supporting me and making sure that I
remained focused on the task at hand, which was getting
your books to you on time. Laughing but dead serious.
To my husband, the perfect verse over a tight beat.
Thanks for being nothing more than you!

**If I have forgotten anyone, know that
I love you still**

TABLE OF CONTENTS

Chapter 1

Chapter 2

Chapter 3

Chapter 4

Chapter 5

Chapter 6

Chapter 7

Chapter 8

Chapter 9

Chapter 10

Chapter 11

Chapter 12

Chapter 1— Cesar

"Mmm. That shit feels so good baby." I moaned leaning back against the wall trying to stay leveled.

I had to admit; she was definitely breaking a nigga down, much like she did every morning before I had to go to work. Not only was it a perfect start to my day but it also kept her cool. This allowed her to think that if she made me bust a couple before I left, I wouldn't want to fuck another bitch. Her insecurities always got the best of her since every man she's ever dealt with in the past had dogged her. I could tell her I'm a different type of man all day and she would still think I was out here chasing down chicks on a regular. It didn't phase me none though. As long as she was in the giving mood, I was damn sure gone receive it.

I cuffed the back of her head in my hand, guiding her along with her motion, encouraging her to swallow my manhood deeper and deeper into her mouth. She liked that shit, said it made her pussy wetter. I felt myself about to bust all in her mouth and since I was about to be late for work, I knew there was no sense in holding it in. I jerked into her mouth like my waist was experiencing a spasm, releasing damn near a cup full of nectar inside of it; watching as she happily swallowed it down gulp after gulp. She started kissing me from my navel on up to my neck, and then reached back giving me a playful smack on my ass.

"Baby, you better gon' before you be late to work." Mink whispered in my ear as she licked her lips and winked her eye before plopping down on the bed.

"I'm on my way out right now. Let me freshin' my shit back up." I said duck walking to the bathroom with my jeans around my ankles.

After I cleaned up, I came back into the room watching as she rolled around on the bed in her thin pink t-shirt and matching panties. Her 32D's sat up nice when she turned on her back and coupled with her thick as thighs, she knew she was the shit. She knew I was mental for her thick eyebrows, brown buttery skin and long video vixen weave. Hell it was 2012 and all the females wore their hair like that but none of them had theirs lain better than my chick. She even rocked it bad at seventeen back when I first met her, back when chicks wasn't even really up on their looks. Mink stood at 5'9" like the models you see on TV but her long legs were more beautiful than every one of those airbrushed chicks and back then she knew how to gallop them like a grown woman.

She lied to me about her age when I pulled up on her in my candy apple red box Chevy on twenties. It was my hustle ride, back when I was in the game hard and she pretended like that shit didn't phase her much. But I went down six months after that, got popped off cause I hit a nigga in the mouth and his bitch ass called the police on me. Before I could get in the wind the police rode up on me, found my dope in the trunk and locked my dumb ass up and all my money, power, and fame slowly drifted away.

Mink held a nigga down in the joint though and my first month there told me she was four months pregnant with my little dude. I've been in love with shorty ever since. A nigga was lucky enough to had only did a three year bid in Cook County but all I could think about was her, from sun up to sun down, she was it. She worked at Burger King just to support a nigga so in my book that was real shit. When I got out and found work eight months later, I gave her any and everything she could ask for. I worked hard and kept my hands clean so I could raise my son, our son. If I could lay up under her all day I would but right now business and money called so I had to go.

"Make sure that thang is nice and sweet when I get home this evening, ya heard me?" I smiled breaking free from my trance while buckling up my pants.

"Isn't it always, Cesar?" Mink replied sarcastically popping her neck. "Um, baby before you go, can I have a few dollars to take CJ shopping? He needs some new shoes before he goes to my mom's house tomorrow. You know he gotta look fly in front of his friends."

"Just take my Chase card and get what you need. I got a couple of dollars for lunch so I'm good." I sighed as I handed her the card before kissing her forehead, snatching my keys, and racing out the door.

Walking out of the six flat court-way building, my thumb hit the unlock button on my '97 Jeep Grand Cherokee before I hopped in revving the engine and pulled off wildly. As I drove, I couldn't help but think about the talk Mink and I had last night. I understood that she was tired of being my baby momma and deserved to be a wife but I just wasn't sure if she was wife material. I would give her the shirt off my back all day but that last name is something that shouldn't be given lightly. Her past indiscretions in the relationship I can forgive but never forget. Shit I've been asking her for seven years for a DNA test to CJ and she still hasn't given me that yet. Regardless of the fact, I still chose to give the little dude my name making him Cesar Jr. I choked it up cause the little nigga looks like me, in the nose and eyes and shit. But I ain't gon' lie the doubt plagues my mind everyday. In my eyes no matter how much she fought the issue, Mink wasn't ready to change her last name from Johnson to King.

Turning right on 47th and Western then pulling into the Home Depot parking lot, I was still thinking about the conversation. Though Mink claimed she was a good woman now, her faults kept ringing in my mind. Just a few years ago, I swear that girl got caught with every Kenan, Kel, and Jason and always with her legs tooted up in the air. So she has to know that I can't just jump into something as important as marriage with her. It was true my feelings for her ran deep enough to call it love so I played the fool for her every time and because I remained true to her pussy, her infidelities cut me deeper.

"Hey, Cesar." Lasha waved seductively to me as I walked in the sliding automatic doors of the store.

"Ay, girl." I winked.

"Johnny looking for you."

"Damn, what he want, Lasha?"

"I don't know but he looked real serious about it. He told me as soon as I seen you to tell you to see him." She replied turning back to her register.

"Aight, then." I said headed back to the boss man's office.

"You eatin' Subway today? I can pick it up for you and we can eat in the break room at the same time as always." She yelled after.

I pretended not to hear her. She had only been at the job six months and ever since we met she had been overfriendly. I mean shorty was fire hot with her short 5'5" stature, bubble round booty and long dark hair. She looked like she was mixed or something cause she had darker skin than any white or Mexican girls I knew but her hair was straight and thin. Her breasts sat on her chest like to firm cantaloupes and she made sure to wear the tightest clothes to work everyday so a nigga would look. I'm a man, not dead, so I looked but never touched even when my Johnson wanted to. Besides my palms were sweaty as hell wondering exactly what this supervisor could have wanted with me.

I'm never really late but today a truck was coming in

and I know he told us to be on time for it. Glancing back towards the freight area I could see the guys all standing around fucking off and smoking squares so I knew the truck hadn't come yet. All I had to do was hump my ass off to finish that truck by 6pm and Johnny would have been all good with me. Hell, I'll take the write-up for being late, that was nothing. I've been working since CJ was born, having quit my gangbanging and dope dealing ways cause my son came first in my life.

"Yo, Johnny. You wanted to see me, bro?" I asked stepping in the door of his office.

"Yeah, Cesar. Thanks for coming in. I needed to talk to you about a few things that just came to my attention this morning." Johnny replied fumbling through the mess of papers that swarmed his small cheap metal desk. "Uh, shut the door would you?"

I looked around pissed that he had even fixed his lips to say that. I squeezed my big 5'9" 200 pound of solid muscle chocolate thunder ass all the way in the cramped office thinking in the back of my head that they desperately needed to invest some money into this shit here. There was literally nowhere for me to sit so I just stood there grasping hold of the straps that hung from the black stretchy back brace I had around my shoulders. The white skin on Johnny's face quickly turned red as he began to shuffle realizing he had no idea what he did with those papers. He ran his fingers through his low buzzed cut and straightened his black square shaped glasses trying to focus. While he worked on that I tucked in my white polo and adjusted my orange smock in an attempt to look presentable before I spoke.

"Ok, before you speak let me first say that I know I was late this morning after you asked us to be on time for the truck. So I just wanna go on record with saying that I'm sorry for that and I accept any consequences that may come behind that, sir." I cleared my throat. "So you can save the speech. I'll just take my write up so I can get right on to work. That is if you don't mind sir."

"Uh, no Cesar. It's not about your tardiness today. It's about your application when you first applied." He said biting the lower half of his cracked lip.

"My application? That was like 7 years ago Johnny, I'm not understanding why that's an issue now." I chuckled using my left arm as an armrest for my other arm while it stroked my thin well-tapered beard.

"Well it looks like you wrote down that you were never convicted of a felony. But that's not true is it?"

"What? Man, I don't even know what you talking about, Johnny. Can I just go start my job, please?" I asked trying to get off that dumb shit he was spitting to me.

"Cesar, corporate wasn't really doing background checks on employees back then. But they had decided last week to check up on all the employees in every city and they got to ours yesterday. I got an email this morning of everyone who needed to be terminated and..."

"Johnny...please don't say what I think you're about to say. Please, man." I sighed heavily.

"I'm sorry, Cesar. If there was anything that I could do, you know I would. You're a hard worker and I'm sorry to see you go but there's nothing that I can do." Johnny replied solemnly.

"Man, I can't believe this shit dude. Seven fucking years and all of a sudden they wanna do their fucking job. I need this job for my son, for my family. What am I supposed to do now?" I felt the anger choke my voice.

"Why'd you lie dude?"

"I didn't lie. I just omitted the truth and I didn't even think it was relevant cause I was nineteen at the time I got locked up and only did two years. They told me I could get it expunged cause it was a minor drug offense so that's what I did." I quickly explained.

"If you got it expunged then it shouldn't have even shown up. Maybe you need to check to see if they approved you and if so then bring those papers in and we can see about getting your job back. But as of right now it looks like you lied and there's nothing I can do for you." Johnny said scratching his Hulk Hogan mustache.

"FUCK!" The words flew from my lips in a torrent I couldn't control.

"I'm sorry man." Johnny lowered his head knowing that was all he could say as I yanked the office door as wide open as I could and stormed out.

It took everything inside of me not to knock them damn papers off his desk and them busted up ass glasses off his face but I knew it wasn't his fault. My feet hit the floor harder than a wrecking ball to a building, thinking about what the fuck could have happened to my expungement paperwork. I know I filled that shit out. My thoughts reflected to the exact moment that I signed them, stuffed them in an envelope then licked them sealed. Either the state of Illinois was on some bullshit or when I handed them to Mink to mail off, she never did. I didn't know but I was

damn sure on my way home to find out and since it was
Monday morning I knew somebody at the state's office in
Springfield, IL was going to feel my wrath.

"Cesar. Cesar, where you going?" Lasha called after
but I pretended not to hear her again. "Wait."

"Lasha, I ain't got time for this shit right now."

"What is it? Maybe I can help." She called after.

I walked on. I was in no mood to smell her sweet
vanilla scent, gaze upon her bronzed skin, or watch her
seductively curl her fingers around her long rich dark hair.
My thoughts wouldn't allow me to focus on her beauty, no
matter how bad my heart wanted to. See, I had a small crush
on her only because she embodied everything in a woman
that Mink didn't so I couldn't help my attraction. She was
worldly exotic from her infectious ear to ear smile to her
mild accent but she would never tell me where she was
from. Thirty minutes on a lunch break everyday was never
really enough time to get to know a person.

But my rage ran too deep to focus on what the hell
she was talking about. As bad as I wanted to stop and oblige
her in conversation and stare into those deep dark brown
eyes, I rushed back through the sliding doors and into the

parking lot. I don't even remember starting the truck I just remember speeding so fast through the stoplights and not even worrying about getting a ticket. That was pure luck though. My key turned in the keyhole as I pushed the door wide open slamming it behind me.

"Mink! Mink, where you at girl?" I yelled tossing my keys on the small round wooden coffee table then pulling my smock above my head, flinging it over on the small plush beige couch. "Mink!"

I knew she heard me. My voice was as loud as ever; a trait that I got from my daddy all those years he used to call me in for dinner from down the street. He had been dead twenty of my twenty-seven years of life; to this day he is still truly missed. It dawned on me to pay attention to my surroundings. The blaring Beyonce cd that she always played while cleaning the house resonated in my brain; that's the reason why she couldn't hear shit. She knew I liked the house *damn* clean when I got home but a clean house was the last thing on my mind at this point.

My hands wrapped around my body in a snug hug before lifting my shirt above my head, revealing my chiseled abs and bulging pecs. It drove her crazy and I would need that distraction to gain sympathy for the fact that I lost my job and we might be broke again for a while. As I passed CJ's room, I looked at the clock on his cable box realizing that I had at least five more hours to bust Mink's back out and calm her down before I picked him up from his second to last day of school. As I walked to our bedroom and opened the door, the sunlight and thick cloud of smoke hit me square in the face like a bomb over Baghdad.

"Mink? Are you fucking kidding me right now?" I spat, feeling a sharp jolt of anxiety shoot through my veins.

"Oh my God! Baby, what are you doing here so early?" She replied jumping up pushing the man's head up from in between her legs.

"Man..." I placed my head in my hand as I smiled to keep from snapping.

"Baby. It's not...he was just...Cesar..." Panic could be heard in her trembling voice.

"Just shut the fuck up, Mink." I said turning my attention to the baldhead R. Kelly looking motherfucka who was frantically searching the room for his clothes and whatever else he stripped off.

The green in the air wasn't covering up the loud ass pussy smell caked in the room. It only meant one thing; he was already outside waiting until I left and came right on in and got to work. I had only been gone a little over an hour and a half but I know Mink; she likes to get her dirt out the way early so there was no room for slip-ups in the end.

"I can't believe you did this shit to me again, man. Again? How many times is that, Mink? Huh? What 7, 8? How many times do you think a nigga is about to put up with this shit, bitch?" It took every fiber of my being not to stomp a big ass sized twelve mud hole in this niggas dome and plant two slugs in this bitch's clit.

"No baby. I'm sorry! I'm so sorry! Please—"

"Please what? Bitch get off me!" I roared as I pushed her clenching arms off of my waist, watching this nigga scramble out of my bedroom then out the front door before I searched hungrily on the shelves of the closet for my .38. "I can't believe this shit! You twenty-five years old with a kid and you still a hoe."

"Cesar, please calm down baby let me explain!" Mink screamed grabbing hold of my leg trying to slow me down.

"Oh now you wanna explain? Ok then, explain how I just found you with this nigga chomping down on ya nasty ass pussy."

"Ugh! You tryin' to make it seem like it's just me with the issues and shit when I know somethin' is going on with you and that bitch Lasha at work. I've seen the way y'all be around each other. Plus I need some action in my life." Mink said crossing her arms as if she had the upper hand. "You always workin' and always tired—"

"And you always spendin' and always cryin'!"

"UGH! Tell me you not fuckin' her then, Cesar! Tell me you not!"

"Who, Lasha? That's all you got? Man, baby you need to come harder than that, for real, if you wanna pin some bullshit like that on me." I replied.

"You know my momma work there too. She be seeing you all up in that bitch's face. What you thought she wasn't gon' tell me?" She laughed.

"Mink you graduated from high school so you can't be that stupid to think I would cheat on you in front of your people. So you can miss me with that shit."

"Nigga you tryin' to be funny?"

"Naw, but you know what's so funny, though?

What's funny is I should have fucked that bitch. Should've made her sweet little pussy scream. Then maybe I wouldn't be so damn mad right now." I turned my back on her ass and headed back into the cramped living room. "Ay, you need to leave. Straight up."

"Leave? Nigga, you got me fucked up, this is my shit. My name is on the lease not yours." Mink sauntered after me snapping.

"But who pays the fucking bills all up and through here? Not your broke ass and I ain't about to have you bussing niggas down in front of my son." My hand rose right along with my voice. "Get the fuck out, Mink. I ain't gon' say it again."

"Where am I supposed to go, Cesar?"

"I don't know." I barked. "Go to Hell for all I care!"

Mink's eyes were watered with con artist tears as she headed her naked body back towards the bedroom, hopefully in search of her fucking clothes and shit so she could get the fuck out. I sat on the couch replaying the morning's events in my head over and over but not before taking out some green and a cigarillo from my stash and rolling it up. Shit was just fucked up; losing my job and my

girl all in the same day. I didn't know what the fuck I was
going to do about it all but it was time that I stopped giving a
fuck about a lot of shit. A nigga was tired of getting his heart
stomped on repeatedly just for an unappreciative money
hungry bitch. I couldn't do nothing but shake my head and
hit the blunt hard inhaling deeply, hoping that I could calm
down before I needed to face my son.

Chapter 2— Mink

"Hey girl. Are you busy?" I whispered as I wiggled my fat ass into my Dereon jeans.

"Naw, girl I'm good 'til tonight. Wassup?" Flava asked groggily sounding as if she had just woken up.

"Girl, I don't know why this nigga came home early but he did and—"

"He caught your dumb ass?"

I don't know how Flava always did that but she always knew what the fuck was going to happen before it ever happened. Ever since we were kids, my momma used to praise her saying she was older and wiser beyond her time. I felt she was the favorite daughter but I tried not to let that fuck up our relationship. When I was younger, I loved her to the fullest but as we grew older that love began to dwindle down. She was smarter, college educated, and spoiled rotten. As for me, I grew up and out gaining a banging body, which gave me the tools to get any man I wanted and milk them dry like cows.

Of course I was waiting on her to throw the 'I told you so' in my face but I just knew I was so slick with my shit. As long as I did my dirt early in the morning that nigga would be none the wiser or so I thought. My plan went unscathed, flawless for years. Guess I never anticipated on him coming home early one day; one day out of seven years. My heart was pounding a mile a minute and honestly I didn't want to leave. I wanted to go in the living room and drop to my knees bobbing and weaving until that nigga forgave me, again.

Yeah I had cheated on him many times before and he would always take me back for the sake of CJ. He was an excellent dad, I had to give it to him and he wanted to keep him in a two-parent home. But a bitch has got needs and if they are not met when I need them to be I'm going to figure out a way to make it happen. Don't get me wrong my baby lays the pipe and his tongue is like hot wet magic but he's always tired cause he works so damn much. Shit, my pussy don't take vacations.

"Can you come and get me?" I begged packing a few things in my Louis Vuitton duffle.

"Damn, Mink. I'm in the bed with my motherfucking husband hoe. Something you don't know shit about. It's too early in the morning for this shit." Flava snapped as I pretended to cry through the phone.

"Please, Flava. I'm so sorry. Tell Yolo that I am so sorry but I need your help girl. I ain' got nowhere else to go and I know momma gon' be trippin' if I go to her house." The lie ran from my lips like water from a faucet. I just really needed to be up under her. "Please."

"Aight. Damn, bitch don't make this no habit."

"Ok, I promise."

"I bet you do. I'll be there in a minute. You know we stay in Schaumburg so you better just sit out front 'til we get there." Flava said.

"Wait we? You bringing, Yolo?" I asked.

"Girl you know I don't go nowhere without that nigga."

"Damn, aight."

As I hung up my cell and stuffed it down into my pocket, I dreaded seeing his fine ass. I wanted him so badly that night they met in the club five years ago but Flava strutted her 5'7" thick waisted ass on over there to him first. Since then, they were inseparable and it pissed me off.

When I found out how he made his money, it made my pussy tingle. Flava's hatin' ass wouldn't hook me up with none of his boys talking about they weren't worthy enough to even talk to,and she was probably right since Yolo was bigger than all of them.

He stood six feet and looked as if he weighed about two hundred solid pounds of muscle. One of those niggas who looked like he had just got out the pen but with none of the actual physical or emotional scars since he had never been. He exuded confidence, the sexiest trait of a man. Word on the street was that he brought his business here from Mexico, where he was born and raised and made a killing more than he ever would have down there. He always rocked braids straight to the back and stayed flashy from his car to his clothes. Every time I thought of him my pussy melted. So when they announced they were getting married the following year after they had met, I wanted to beat the fuck out of her. Then they got married within three months of the fuckin' announcement! She knew I saw him and wanted him first but she went on and married this nigga anyway. Secretly, I never forgave her for that. But she was my sister and I had to let it go. Still, that nigga's face drove me crazy.

I finished stuffing a few more sexy panties into my

bag then snatched it up, even as heavy as it was. Struggling with the bag, I headed back into the living room tossing it on the floor next to the front door. Cesar's sexy ass was lying back on the couch blowing one back and staring up at the ceiling. I still couldn't believe his ass put me out of *our* apartment. The skin on his chest looked like hot melted dark chocolate with his bare chest flexing every time he put the blunt to his full succulent lips. I was getting wet just thinking about not being able to have this nigga anymore. There was no way I was about to let this man walk out of my life; especially since we had a son together. Naw, he had to forgive me whether he liked it or not.

"Can I smoke with you one last time?" I asked sweetly.

He didn't even speak, just handed me the blunt as I took a seat next to him on the couch. We didn't have much in our cozy humble abode with a 32" TV screen sitting on a flimsy stand next to the hall wall that I had been desperately trying to get him to upgrade. The wall next to the front door was littered with family photos of our not so happy family, almost fifty pictures hung there in a decorative motif. I was a photo queen. The large plastic bamboo floor plants set a soothing Feng Shui backdrop for relaxation. If I could do nothing else, I could cook, fuck, and decorate. Our apartment was small and our things were not of the highest quality but it was ours and I wasn't about to let him just throw it all away.

"Baby you gotta forgive me. I don't know why I do the things I do." I lied. "But I need you. You're the only one who can help me get over this and make me a better person."

"Naw. You don't need me, you just want me. There's a difference. You need to get your priorities straight, Mink."

"I know baby. I don't know what I be thinking sometimes. You're a good man that's why I pamper you the way I do."

"Hmph." He shrugged as he passed me the blunt back.

"Ugh, tell me what I can do to make this better baby. I wanna stay here with you and our son. I wanna work on us." I pleaded watching his demeanor closely.

Cesar didn't budge much the entire time. He reached his hand down in between his legs adjusting his piece and replanting his Timbs firmly back on the floor. Damn, he was looking sexy in his Home Depot attire and I just had to have him. My hand seemed to have a mind of its own as it danced over to his strong thigh; massaging it roughly. He still hadn't budged, I knew he wanted to makeup but he wouldn't be his self if he didn't act stubborn about it.

"What are you doing, Mink?" Cesar asked hitting the blunt.

"I think it's time we made up, baby. Remember we said never to go to bed mad." I replied unzipping his pants, struggling to get them off of his waist.

"That shit ain't gon' fix us girl. Not anymore."

"I know but it's a start."

He was obviously not going to help me resolve this but I wasn't about to stop not even if he told me to. Reaching my hand down into his pants, I grabbed hold of the massive sized beef within. It was very limp but even still it carried weight. He was a man with big hands, big feet, and a big long tongue. It was only appropriate that his dick followed suit. I loved it when it wasn't hard because it flopped in and out of my mouth like a fish out of water. Releasing it gently from his cage, I slid my mouth far down on it before he had the chance to deny me the act.

"Mmm." He moaned scooting down on the couch relaxing even further.

"You like that daddy?" I asked popping his dick out of my mouth long enough to speak before swallowing it whole again.

Cesar didn't respond. I knew he did though. He once dubbed me "Golden Jaws" because I could suck a mean dick at the drop of a hat. I credit my expertise to years of watching the chicks on the porno flicks get it in the way they did. With my right hand, I squeezed the bottom of it stroking up and down in the same motion as my mouth, careful not to scathe it with my teeth. Niggas don't like toothy ass brain. Cesar was indeed growing in my mouth. With my other hand, I reached inside of my jeans rubbing my clit as I felt him reach down to play with my left nipple; getting it nice and erect. Shit, I was about to cum. I loved it because it made me go ham on his dick even more. My mouth sucked nicely on the head of his beef while I stroked the bottom half rapidly.

"Ooo, shit!" He bellowed.

It was his time. I wanted that cum all inside of my mouth, ready to swallow it down so I could jump up on this hard junk and ride it 'til the wheels fell off. My head was bobbing so hard I thought I was going to get whiplash at some point but being determined there was no way I was going to give up. Cesar's body began jerkin' like he wanted to explode in my mouth but in that split second his dick just went limp. Whay the fuck? I worked like hell trying to get it back up, sucking feverishly and tonguing so much that my shit went numb but he wouldn't get back up for me.

She ain't fuckin' wit you unless you

Got a lotta money

Got a lotta

Got a lotta money

Damn. I had been meaning to change that fucking ring tone for the longest but Diamond was my girl. She was a real rapper and I loved her style.

"Ha ha. You better gon' and get your phone girl." Cesar laughed as he took the duct of the blunt setting it down in the ashtray like nothing had ever happened.

"Fuck that damn phone, baby." I said allowing his dick to flop out of my mouth.

"Naw, gon' and get it." His voice was very calm, almost a scary calm.

It pissed me off but there was nothing left for me to

do once he snatched his beef tucking it back down in his pants like he was done with me. I couldn't believe he didn't cum, it was the first time he had ever went limp in my mouth beforehand.

"WHAT?" I screamed angrily into the phone.

"Bitch you better calm that bass down in your voice and get your ass out here. We outside." Flava responded.

"Oh girl, damn. My bad, I forgot."

"Well are you coming or not?"

"Um, naw, Flav. I think I'm gonna stay here and work on my relationship with my baby's daddy." I said sounding as if I was explaining things to her for the first time while I turned to catch his nonchalant reaction.

"Girl you had me drive all the way to the city to get your punk ass and you flakin'? I tell you what, the next time something goes on with you, don't call me. How about that?" Flava replied halfheartedly.

"I said my bad, Flav, dang."

"You just come and open this door, cause we're here now. No sense in jumping right back on the road." She replied, as a gentle knock was present at the door.

Cesar had finished buttoning up his pants before I opened the door letting Flava and Yolo inside. I dipped off to the bathroom really quickly to wash the sex aroma from my hands and face before returning to get a whiff of that strong tantalizing smell emanating from Yolo's body. I could never for the life of me figure out where to buy that cologne from for Cesar. I wanted him to smell just like that every day, so I could feel like I had a small piece of Yolo around me at all times. He and Cesar were chatting it up heavy when I came back into the room, not allowing Flava and me to get a word in edgewise. Flava sat in the recliner next to the couch on Yolo's side, leaning in towards him as if to always remain as close as possible to him.

Even at 9am in the morning, Flava's makeup stayed flawless, her hair was always laid, and her nails were always done immaculately. I always envied her wardrobe, never rocking anything that cost less than $200. In fact, the salmon colored Ekaterina short jumper that fit her body like a glove made me green. I tried to keep up with her but on Cesar's budget that shit was not happening the way I wanted it to. People always mistook us for twins though she was two years older than me. I copied everything she did because I wanted her lifestyle. I used to be in denial about it but fuck it, it was true. She had natural long dark hair down to the small of her back and I had short shoulder length hair so I went out and bought me some hair. Her waist was small while her hips were beautiful child bearing ones, so I went to the gym and asked a personal trainer to kick my body into gear. I sometimes think I could actually pass for her if it weren't for one thing, she had Yolo and I didn't.

She ain't fucking with you unless you...

"Damn, it's momma." I grimaced before moving to the bedroom to get away from the loud male bonding voices. "Hey ma."

"Hey Mink. How's my grandson?"

"Momma he's fine. Why you always calling here asking about him first? Hello, I am your daughter."

"Yeah, yeah but you grown. I ain't gotta worry about you no more." My momma chuckled. "So what's going on with you and that boy?"

"Ugh, momma you know his name. Just like he knows your name, Ms. Pearl. But we are fine." I said shaking my head at the fact that after all these years of proving her wrong she still didn't like Cesar.

"Well you know Flava called me and told me what

was going on. Why you can't seem to keep your legs closed, I'll never know. That was the problem I had with you when you was younger; always sneakin' out the damn window..."

"Ma! Is that what you called for? To shit on me?"

"Nope, that ain't it. I called to see if that boy told you what happened at work today." She paused.

"No, momma. What happened?"

My heart dropped. I just knew she was going to tell me that someone had caught Cesar fucking that bitch at his job. I knew she was going to tell me they had been fucking for some time so I could go back in the other room and whoop his ass for trying to make me look like the only big hoe in the house. But when she explained that he had lost his job because he lied on his job application seven years ago, I was beyond livid.

"Ma, let me call you back."

"Yeah, well are you still sending CJ over here for the summer when he gets out of school this weekend?" She asked sounding as if she was nibbling on some food, sending obnoxious smacking noises through the phone.

"Yes momma. You will have your boy all summer." I

laughed but was more than grateful that she loved my son enough to take him every summer.

"Yay! Ok, hit me back." She said before hanging up.

I wanted to love my mother, but sometimes she pissed me off. We only seemed to bump heads when she brought up my past or was trying to be funny and talk shit about my life. But since being grown, she had become more of a friend than a mother and with both of us out of the house she had started getting her groove back and trying to sound hip these days. More importantly, I was proud that she had lost a hundred pounds in a year and was now forty-seven, sexy and fabulous releasing her inner hoe; even though she had only been seeing one guy since she got skinny. My smile quickly deteriorated though, when I thought about the info she had told me, as I headed back into the room to question him about it. The only thing that kept running through my head was the fact that we would be broke and that was something that I was not prepared to tolerate.

"Cesar, can I speak with you in the other room for a second please?" I asked placing my hands on my hips.

"No." He replied in a deep assertive voice turning back to his conversation with Yolo.

"Fine. Why the fuck you ain't tell me that you got fired today?" I blurted.

"You got fired?" Flava screeched.

"Damn dog that's fucked up." Yolo spat, rolling the blunt licking the final flap with his sexy ass moist tongue.

I had to focus. "So answer the question."

"Yeah. I got fired today. Tell ya moms I said thanks for minding her own damn business." He replied sarcastically.

"What the fuck did you do, Cesar? How we gon' live? How we gon' eat? I'll be damned if I go down to the aid office and have my baby eating off of food stamps." I said folding my arms angered by his stupidity.

"Shit you gon' have to do what you have to do then and get your ass off your shoulders. Beggars can't be choosey." Cesar said slouching down further into the couch.

"I'm not begging, motherfucka."

"Then why don't you get a fucking job then, Mink? CJ is in school all day that's more than enough hours for you to work." He snapped. "And ya moms got him all summer so you barely have him anyway."

"Yeah, sis. It is about time for you to get a job too. Shit I can't remember the last time you worked. I think Burger King was your last spot." Flava chimed in.

"I can't work because my son needs me here and I got that medical condition." I retorted.

Laughter broke out around the room. I watched as all of them rolled hard at my expense. "What the fuck is so funny?"

"What condition you got, Mink? Allergies from hard work?" Cesar busted out as the group continued to laugh.

"NO! I...I have leg problems." I said as they all laughed harder than ever now.

"Anyway, I wouldn't even be in this shit if you would've just mailed my motherfucking paperwork to get my drug case expunged back then." The look in Cesar's eyes grew dark and evil. "The one thing I asked you to do and you couldn't even do that."

I had never seen him so angry not even at the other times he had caught me cheating on him in the past. Thinking back I tried to piece together what actually happened to that damned envelope he gave me to mail off but I couldn't. My palms were so sweaty that I could have watered the grass with them. I didn't know what to say to him or how to respond to that. I was wrong and I knew it.

"I did mail it off, Cesar." I lied. "It ain't my fault if the state didn't do its damn job." I crossed my arms and plopped down on the beanbag chair in between the couch and the TV in the corner.

"Ay man. I don't know what you plan on doing for money but you're always welcomed to my hustle." Yolo spat turning to Cesar.

When I heard those words roll of his sweet succulent lips, my eyes lit up like a kid in a toy store. Yolo and Flava needed and wanted for nothing and if I could get a piece of that I would be the happiest girl in the world. Never again would we be broke or have to worry about the bills and rent being paid. Never again would my son have to beg Cesar for the things that he wants, he could have everything his little heart desired. I focused on Yolo's long dark braids then his rich sun-tanned skin. Flava was damn lucky and a part of me felt like she didn't deserve it, didn't deserve him.

"Yolo, as tempting as that does sound, I'm gonna have to pass. Been on the up and up for a long time now, ain't really tryin' to go back." Cesar replied noticing the dismay on my face as he spoke.

"Com' on now dude you know I ain't gon' have you out there bogus like that and all my shit is tight, straight up. I've been doing this for a minute so it's gotta stay tight, ya feel me?" Yolo said as he rose reaching his hand out to help Flava from her seat, not that she needed it.

"Yeah. I feel you. Thanks though." Cesar said checking out Flava's ass as she turned and walked towards the door.

"Aight dude. You change your mind, you know how to holla at me." Yolo replied shaking up with Cesar before heading to the door. "Bye, Mink."

"Bye. Thanks for coming by." I replied as I watched what should've been my future walk out the damn door.

As I closed the door, I couldn't stop replaying over and over again the words that Yolo said. Cesar could make our lives complete. That penny pinching he was doing back in the day is nothing compared to the big money I know he can make up under Yolo. All he needed to do was swallow his pride and get the fuck in the ring.

"So Cesar—"

"No Mink."

"But Cesar, if you just listen to reason—"

"NO MINK!" Cesar thundered as he walked off to the bathroom slamming the door behind me.

Chapter 3— Cesar

For the last seven days, Mink hasn't been able to drop the offer that Yolo extended me last week. Yesterday I almost hit her in the jaw for even fixing her lips to ask again. I saw a devilish grin of greed underneath her pity party facial expressions dance across her face each time. But she could hang it up though. My drug selling days were over and there was not a chance in hell I'd go back and risk my freedom and not be able to see Cesar Jr. again.

I dressed in my fresh Calvin Klein gray colored suit, compliments of a sale at Burlington Coat Factory. My shoes were of a patent leather and a name I knew nothing of. I shaved clean just for the occasion and moisturized my face for that added shine and glow to my face. I was cleaner than that thang feeling like nobody could tell me anything or say no to a face like this.

"Awe shit now! Look who's all sexy today. What's the occasion?" Mink asked stopping by the bathroom.

"Shit a nigga is about to go get a job and I ain't coming home until I do." I replied putting the finishing touches on my smooth dark skin.

"Oh." She grimaced as she continued her journey to the living room. "Well you'll have to take the bus where you're going cause I have to take CJ some more clothes for the summer to my mom's. He's going to be next door with his little friend Kyle and they're gonna be doing stuff so..."

"So what? You can't give me a ride nowhere or nothing?"

"You know what baby I would love to but they are going to the aquarium soon and I don't wanna make them late." She replied pretending to rush through the house looking for nothing.

"And what are you doing after that?"

"Oh, I've gotta run my momma to work because her car is down right now."

It was clear that she was digging herself into a hole trying not to drive me around to go job hunting. But I was feeling too good and in too good of a mood to let her ass blow my natural high. She grabbed the big red rollaway suitcase sitting in the middle of the living room dragging it to the front door.

"Okay hun I'm gone. Don't wait up I might be going out with Flava and the girls later." She said as she walked out the door.

She didn't even say goodbye. This bitch had the nerve to be acting like she was mad at me when she was the one caught with her legs in the air. Fuck that shit. I searched for the business folder I had created last night that held my resumes and forklift certification and headed out. My feet hit the pavement harder than an elephant, ready to get the day started and conquer this job search. As I approached the bus stop on the corner, I felt a little less than a man. I felt as if a piece of my manhood had been chopped off and burned never to return. For the most part, I choked this up as miniscule depression.

Honk! Honk!

"Hey Cesar. You need a ride?" Lasha asked pulling up in front of me in her nearly ten year old gold convertible Sebring.

"Hell yeah!" I replied, no shame in my game.

"Damn that's crazy seeing you on the bus stop. Where you gotta go?" Lasha asked as I slid into the passenger's seat.

"Shit just job hunting. Tryin' to keep my paper flowin'. You can take me to Chicago Ridge if you can. I figure all them damn stores in that mall, somebody is bound to say yes. Ya know?"

"Yeah I feel you. So how's ya girl doing?" Lasha asked as I looked over noticing how thick her thighs seemed in those jeans.

"She's cool." I licked my lips.

I could tell she was on her way to work because she had her orange smock and polo sitting right on the armrest. It was so hot outside that she wore only a tight red tank top that hugged her tits nicely; sitting upright, teasing me as they bounced gently with every bump on the road. It was hard not to look at the golden melons glistening in the sun and every time she looked over to see what I was gawking at I played it off like I was checking out something past her.

"Hmm. Well we're still friends Cesar. We've known each other for enough months to call each other friends and since I started that bitch ass job you've been more than nice to me. So if you ever need to talk or anything, you can always call me." Lasha licked her honey brown full lips slowly taking my Iphone out of my hand at the stoplight to type her number in.

She called her phone to have my number in her phone as well and even though I should've objected to the whole thing, I didn't. Shit that number might come in handy one day since I know she's willing to help a nigga in need out. I reached in my pocket pulling out a dub, waving it to her.

"I wanna thank you for helping me out. You probably gon' be late for work by doing this but I do appreciate you." I said still waving the money by her side.

"Oh my God. If you don't put that shit away, Cesar. I don't want nor do I need your money." She replied turning up her lips.

"Ok but gas ain't cheap and nothing comes free, girl. It's out of respect so just take it."

"I don't want your money Cesar...I want your time. I want you, baby." Lasha whispered softly side eyeing me to see if I heard her. I did.

"Lasha, you know my situation. I'm just not that type of man-"

"I know. That's probably why I'm so attracted to you." She sighed. "You ain't gotta say nothing and if you give me that money you'll only hurt my feelings. Just consider it a friend helping a friend."

Lasha slapped me on my knee playfully, laughing to cover her true feelings as she pulled into the mall parking lot. Baby girl was feeling me harder than I thought she was. I knew she liked me but something inside of me told me it reached a little bit deeper than just a simple crush. I'm not gonna front. I might have led her on a tad bit with it as well but it was only because I felt shit wasn't right at home and a part of me felt it too. I felt bad for Lasha, loving a nigga who was unavailable, but she was a good person and I didn't want to hurt her.

"Well, here you go. Good luck baby." Lasha smiled shooting me a good-humored punch in the arm.

"Thanks again, girl." I said slipping the dub back down into my pocket while getting out the car, folder in hand. "I truly appreciate you."

"It's nothing baby. Call me anytime." Lasha winked her right eye at me.

She pulled off and I walked inside the mall, checking my phone for the time, 9:22am. The shop signs were all brightly lit and the floors were newly polished and the halls were deserted since the mall had just opened a few minutes ago. It was the perfect time to speak to managers before the customers came rushing in with money to spend. The entire time I stood in the middle of the hall trying to figure out which store to hit first, I could think of nothing but Lasha. Her kindness, smooth skin, and the fact that she was willing to do anything for a nigga raised my awareness about her. Not to mention, shorty had a badass body.

I walked into Footlocker noticing that none of the employees greeted me or even acknowledged that I was there. Working in retail for as long as I did, I knew exactly how to play this.

"Excuse me. May I speak to the manager please?" I asked from across the room keeping one eye on them and the other on the one customer they had in the store.

I walked right up to the customer and introduced myself as a potential employee and asked him if he needed any help. I was poised and confident knowing that I knew any and everything that had to do with running shoes, especially the AirMaxes that he was in the vicinity of. Every question that the old balding Caucasian man spat out at me I spat an answer right back, laughing and sharing old war stories as men did in this situation. I have laughed and conversed with many great customers on a regular basis so talking with this guy was like second nature.

"Hi, how are you? My name is Paul and I'm the manager here. What can I do ya for?" Paul asked with a bubbly smile, shaking my hand but interrupting what I had going on.

"Paul, this man is here for a job and he just sold me two pairs of AirMaxes. You got a long term customer in me if I can come in here and talk to this young man when I shop." The old man smiled as he winked at me.

"Thank you sir." I smiled back confident that this shit was in the bag.

"Well. I appreciate that sir. Thank you very much." Paul responded before turning to me. "How the hell did you do that? That man comes in here every month and every month he buys nothing."

"When you work for one of the hugest hardware stores known to man for nearly a decade you get to know how to upsell and handle customers." I replied in banter.

"Well I must admit, I'm damn well impressed. Com' on back and talk to me in my office, Mr. uh?"

"King. Cesar King, sir."

"Nice. Well step on back here sir and let's see what we could do about getting you a place here at FootLocker." Paul smiled leading me back to his office.

A sense of pride came over me as I followed him to the back of the store past the three mean mugging employees. Then we past the inventory room and into his small cramped office. I don't know what it was about retail stores but for the most part, the managers all had linen closets for offices. It showed how much the company wanted to invest in their workers. Anyway as he offered me a seat at his desk while he stood, he reached above me on the shelf pulling down an envelope full of new hire paperwork.

"Fill this out for me my man and I'll be back to discuss a few things with you." Paul said gleaming from ear to ear.

"Will do, sir. Thank you."

My fingers were anxious to snatch the papers out of the long white envelope and begin filling in my information. As I skimmed through the papers to become familiar with what I would be answering, I came across that dreaded question. The question that pissed me off the more I read it, the one that had caused all of my problems in the first place.

Have you ever been convicted of a felony?

Why the fuck did they have to ask these questions like this on job applications? I mean, if I tell them I'm a felon they're likely to look at me as an automatic threat to society and shun me from existence. If I lie, just to get honest work , they'll assume I've been scheming all along and condemn me once it's found out . You're damned if you do and damned if you don't with this kind of shit and then they wonder why motherfuckas end up right back in the prison system. Because society refuses to accept them as human beings who still need to support themselves and their families.

Damn!

All I could think about was how my fucking son was gonna eat if I didn't find a job soon. That no good for nothing bitch of mines wasn't gonna get up off her ass and do shit besides, I'm a man. I need to provide for my family. The question stared back at me like I was in a six-man line up at the police station. I knew it was a long shot but I had to take it. My son was counting on me and there was no way I was gonna let my little man down and have him thinking his daddy wasn't shit, wasn't able to take care of him and his momma.

No.

I finally answered that bitch ass question. All I could do was hope they didn't do background checks. I continued on with the rest of my paperwork, filling out every other answer like a breeze. I neatly fixed the work and folded my hands waiting on Paul to return. His office was a reflection of him and another manager whose pictures were plastered on the wall on brown plaques. I could see they were men who took pride in their work having been here for over twenty years.

"Hey buddy. You finished?" Paul said pushing the door open.

"Yes sir. I think so."

"Alrighty, let's have a look." Paul smiled as he took my papers and leaned up against the door.

He barely skimmed through my application before he hovered over my resume. I could see his interest in my resume displayed on his face, probably surprised to see that a black man graduated high school with a 3.5 gpa. Then again he was probably wondering why I was at Home Depot for so many years but never got a damn promotion. I used to wonder that same shit myself.

"Okay, everything looks good." He lied setting the

papers down after barely reading them. "So, how's about you sign this form so I can get the background check underway and while you're doing that I can write you a ticket so you can go take the drug test. We have a clinic in Oaklawn, so it's not that far away."

Paul handed me the form as if he was rushing to finish the paperwork and get me out of there. I think he was so impressed with my floor presentation that he didn't care about much else. But when both of these results came back, I knew Paul would no longer be one of my friends. The pen lay stagnant in my hand as I hesitated to sign my name on that paper. I just couldn't see wasting my time or his knowing that I wouldn't get the job either way.

"Listen, Paul. I need to be honest with you because I know it will spare both of us a lot of grief." My eyes focused in on my shiny shoes, watching a distorted view of my reflection. "I have a felony that was supposed to be expunged but the state never processed my paperwork seven years ago."

"Oh...well I'm sorry guy there's nothing I can do for you here. Good luck in your search though." Paul threw down the pen faster than he turned to open the door for me.

The man heard my truth and it seemed like he

couldn't wait to get rid of me, meaning less forms he needed to process. I stood searching his eyes for any bit of sympathy wondering if I could work my angle over on the man, seeing as though he did see what I was capable of. But the look in his eye let me know that my skills and level of expertise simply just weren't enough.

"Thank you for your time sir." I said as he held the door for me as I walked out. "Oh, and you might wanna get your employees to get up off their asses and actually greet their customers when they come into the store. Just a thought."

"I appreciate that. Have a nice day." Paul's sendoff was cold and as I walked out the door it sounded as if he had slammed it behind me.

One rejection after the other poured into my lap as I damn near hit every store in the entire mall. Not one of those assholes would hire me because of my felony, no matter how long ago or honest I was. There was no use in me lying about it anymore. Nowadays everybody did background checks even McDonalds. Having pounded the pavement all day, I decided to head home. It was going on 4pm and I was beyond tired and more than frustrated, not to mention I had no more resumes left.

I never let you down, I'ma shine on sight

Keep your mind, on your grind, and off of mine's alright? Right…

"Hello?" I answered my Iphone.

"Hey Pop."

"Little man! Whassup boi boi. You over there minding your grandma?" I replied grinning heavily.

"Yeah, Pop. You know she gon' dig in my butt if I don't." CJ chuckled but he wasn't lying though.

Mink's mother, Ms. Pearl, was no push over in her old age. Her driver's license said one age but her face showed a totally different one. She looked like she was twenty-five and was in impeccable shape. My son loved going over there not just for the summer but also for his little friends whose mothers let them roam the streets at all times of days and nights. I didn't condone it but my boy was a good ten year old kid and usually followed his own lead.

"Pop, I was calling to ask if I could have $200 to go to Wisconsin Dells with Hector."

"Who is Hector? The Mexican kid next door to your grandma?"

"Yeah, Pop." He chuckled.

Honestly I didn't have $200 to spare. I needed to preserve all the little money I had left to be able to pay one more month of bills and rent before we started getting in the red, and unable to pay shit. How did I explain to this kid who has always been good and done what we've asked of him, that I couldn't afford to give him what he wanted anymore? I couldn't look him in the eye anymore and call myself a man, his father. A part of me felt like a failure and it resonated all through my voice.

"When you need it by?" I asked hoping he gave me the right answer.

"Next Friday. Grandma says she'll take me shopping for some clothes if I come up with the money to go out there." The happiness in his voice shattered my soul knowing he had his heart set on this trip.

"Alright boy. Call me in a few days to remind me. Okay?" My voice cracked.

"Thanks Pop! Love you!"

"Love you too, son. Now gone and get washed up for dinner."

Once my finger touched that end button, my heart dropped about two feet under the ground. Raindrops slowly dripped onto my screen as I quickly tucked my phone inside of my pants pocket hoping the bus would cross the light before it started to pour down hard. Unfortunately, I had to get the bus that was driving Ms. Daisy rather than the Freddy Kruger bus. The storm kicked in with full force, pouring down within seconds. There was nowhere to run or hide and there was no one else around me, no one to share a fucking umbrella with. The sky grew dark grey as if it was churning in the night scene followed by roaring thunder and flashing lightning.

Finally the Pace bus rolled its happy go lucky slow ass in front of me, whisking open the doors just as slow. I boarded looking up into the driver's face noticing that he was a bald black dude about my age busting his lips over the phone hollering at some broad who he probably wasn't even banging. He looked at me then smirked with his bad breath and gold front plate in his mouth and shrugged as I headed to the back of the very empty bus. The scowling look on my face let dude know not to look back at me since I was beyond heated. It killed me that worthless motherfuckas got jobs and didn't appreciate them but people who were willing to bust their ass for the measly buck never get a chance to.

Chapter 4— Mink

"Girl he won't even talk to me about it. I tried to tell him but he's hard headed. You know how niggas are. Their pride won't let them ask for help for shit." I whined to Flava.

"Well girl you know your man and if he wants to stay legit then what's wrong with that? I mean my man is legit too. He just knows how to work his angles. No man wants to be a bum all his life." Flava spat back at me.

"Ugh, but we broke as hell Flava. I ain't been shopping in a week. A week, girl!" I laughed. "A bitch ain't been able to get her nails or toes did let alone get my weave fixed. Can I borrow some money 'til we get back on our feet?"

"Ah, see now bitch you trippin'. I wouldn't feel comfortable lending you money that's for anything other than rent without a job. Speaking of which, what's wrong with you getting up off your lazy ass to find one? Your man has held you down all these years, even when he was locked up now it's time for you to return the favor." She replied sternly.

"I hate when you try to spit knowledge at me, bitch. I ain't call you for all that, damn. Why can't you just support what I do?" I asked becoming more heated with the conversation.

"Because, Mink, you're wrong. Whether you're my sister or not wrong is wrong and I don't condone that shit. I love you dearly but bitch you need to quit being lazy and get up and get a job." Flava spat as she popped her gum through the phone.

"Ugh, I gotta go. I think I hear Cesar coming in the door."

"Yeah, I'm getting my hair curled anyway 'cause Yolo's taking me out to dinner tonight and we ain't got no kids so you know what that means." Flava laughed like a hyena in my ear. "Bye!"

When I heard the click, I secretly wished it were a guillotine chopping off that bitch's head. Yeah, I was jealous of her but it was for good reason. That bitch didn't deserve to live the good life while I was sitting here near homelessness. She had a college degree in Social Work and could go and get a good ass job where as I only graduated high school and was probably only qualified enough to work at Burger King...again. I didn't give a fuck about that type of shit though, cause while she was held hostage in somebody's school for four years I was getting my party on. Still, it seemed Flava rubbed her lifestyle in my face, which cut like a razorblade from ear to ear.

"Hey." Cesar muttered when I trotted out the room.

"Hey, baby. So, how was the search?" I asked in the sweetest voice.

"Well...it was good practice." He sighed.

If I wasn't depressed from the initial shock of the news, it was slowly creeping up on me. Not being able to shop was hard enough but to sit around and deal with a mopey man was unacceptable. My brain was skating a mile a minute trying to figure out what I could do, leaving him was not an option because I know he would never leave CJ.

"So, do you have a plan on what we're gonna do?" I asked taking a seat next to him on the couch as he began to strip out of his suit.

"What *we're* gonna do? *We* ain't gonna do nothing cause you are too lazy to get out here and get a damn job." He snarled scooting further across the couch away from me.

"I told you I can't work." I fidgeted.

"Yeah whatever—"

"But have you given anymore thought to Yolo's offer?" I interrupted noticing the aggravation growing within him. "I spoke to Flava today and she told me that he really wants you on his team and would even pay you more than he pays his top men just because you're family."

"But I ain't family."

"Yeah but you're like family though. We've all been knowing each other for years now, Cesar, don't be like that." I replied loving caressing his leg.

The storm outside the window was fierce with the howling wind and the beating rain but it was nothing compared to the one brewing inside of him right then. I couldn't figure out what he was actually thinking but I tried to keep my voice as calm as possible in his fragile condition.

"Mink, I ain't trying to go back to dumb shit alright? SO just drop it." He exhaled leaning his head back on the couch as he blew back a brown one. "I'm done with that shit. Why can't anyone understand that?"

"I'm just saying you see how hard it is for you to find a decent job out here that's gonna support an entire family with bills and rent, especially with you being a felon. This shit

is only gonna get harder, Cesar. How much money do we
have left?" I had never had to ask how much money we had
before.

I would ask for a certain amount of money or for a
specific thing and Cesar would be the man of the house and
go out and get it or hand me the money. He never
questioned me and I never questioned him. All of the bills
and rent was always paid on time without fail and with all of
the extra hours he was pulling at Home Depot he made it all
work for us. But it was crunch time and if I was gonna help
fix this it was time I got involved in the expenses.

"Enough to get us through another month." He
replied shaking his head in disappointment.

"See, baby. One more month and then what? Fuck
you and me but what is your son gonna do for food and you
know he's gonna come to you eventually for something?" I
could see him side eyeing me with every word I spoke but
the more he sighed the more I knew, he had to break
eventually. "Before my daddy died, he used to say that a
man is only as good as his family eats."

His head turned to me slightly shooting a piercing
eye my way. It was then that I knew that it was no use. All of
the badgering in the world wouldn't change this nigga's

mind. He was so stubborn that he would eat dirt before he took anyone's advice or maybe just mine. I know that I hurt him bad with all of my cheating but it was what I needed in order to stay happy in this unhappy relationship. The thrill, the sensuality, and the beginning relationship love that I felt with him was gone forever it seemed. I just needed to get that back somehow and since I wasn't going to get it from him, it needed to be from somewhere. I just know that next time I need to be more careful with my game and not let him catch me.

As we sat in silence, I thought about taking my son and running away to a place where he couldn't find us. That way I could have my son and still be rid of him. I mean, we weren't married so it pissed me off that I felt trapped in this relationship. Still, I loved the thought of him and we had been together for so long that I was just so confused. Cesar is the type of man to put his kids before any woman and has told me during many of our fights that I could go wherever I wanted but I was going without CJ. That's something that I'm not prepared to do. A mother living her life carefree without her son is crazy. Right?

"Your daddy was a good man." Cesar finally uttered softly.

"You know he was, I talk about him all the time." I laughed. "Look, I'm just trying to help you better us. I mean, I love you baby. I just want what's best for us, just like you do."

"I know you do." He replied putting the duct in the ashtray, checking his fingers for burns.

"Baby, I'm sorry for hurting you." I said as I leaned in gently to kiss his lips.

I was mildly surprised when he kissed me back. After days of living like roommates and barely speaking to each other, he had finally given in to me. He ran his strong hand across my shirt and over my tits thumbing my nipples one after the other trying to get them as hard as they would go. For the first time in a long time I felt a tingling in my pussy from his touch. It was what I missed from him, what I yearned for. After he started working all those long shifts our sex life went from wild and spontaneous to hum drum quickies. We didn't notice we had a problem until it was too late.

Cesar ran his hand down my smooth belly massaging my skin relieving the tension that had built up within. I felt almost as if a weight was lifted off my shoulders, feeling that we were about to put ourselves, our relationship back together.

"Open your eyes," he whispered. "See what's in front of your face."

My eyes focused in on every single pore of his skin. I looked into his dark eyes before he moved his lips down to my neck, kissing as he laid me down on the couch, securing his hand under the small of my back so I'd go back with ease. I couldn't help but grasp hold to his bulging shoulders, getting a handful of each because of how broad they were. I loved it. Every bit of his body was beautifully crafted, like a masculine piece of fine art. I loosened his dark blue tie then began unbuttoning his all white Oxford, needing to get a glimpse of his carved chest and suck on his brunette nipples.

Once Cesar got wind of my trying to strip him, he grabbed my wrists forcefully pushing them down beside me. He lifted my t-shirt above my breasts revealing their brown loveliness poking out from the top of my green lace bra. It was his favorite color. Immediately, he began trying to devour them; playfully biting and using his teeth to unveil my nipples. When he found them, my soul literally melted as his tongue rolled across them giving light, sensual tickles. He moaned as he sucked them, scrolling simultaneously from left to right to give each of them his undivided attention.

"Get up." He demanded leaving me breathless as I did what he asked.

With one knee on the couch and his other foot planted on the floor, he unbuckled his pants to release his chocolate serpent. My mouth waited for it kneeling down getting ready without him having to ask me to do it. I was ready. Sucking dick? It was nothing to me and I considered myself a professional. I didn't like to do half ass fake jobs like most chicks, only wanting to get their man hard enough to bang their backs out. Nope, that wasn't me. I need to feel the cum squirt into my mouth and roll down the back of my throat. I needed to feel the head beat against my windpipe. It was like an addiction and I was most definitely hooked. The problem was I didn't give a shit whose dick it was as long as there was one in my mouth. That's another area where Cesar and I go wrong.

"You better suck the black off this motherfucka if you want me to forgive you this time." He puffed as he stroked the long limp cock in his hand. "I'm saying that shit better be some super head."

"Whatever you say, baby." I replied eagerly and seductively, jumping into position.

I wrapped my hands around his piece and

interlocked my fingers squeezing firm but remaining tender.
I placed my mouth on him, keeping it open as wide as it
would go; only allowing my tongue to scathe it, moistening it
for my hands. As my hands went down so did my mouth;
both moving in a half circular direction from left to right. His
leg was trembling, that was sign number one that I had him. I
tightened my lips as I motioned up and down permitting
them to give an extra oral massage. More saliva filled up in
my mouth but rather than swallow it, I let it ooze out of my
mouth like a leaky faucet using it as a natural lubrication.

"Ooo, shit!" He bellowed and puffed.

That was sign number two. I continued on with
bobbing and pleasuring him from every angle. I would
release his piece, propping it up to get a good suck on his
balls before returning to the main junk and going to work on
it every five minutes. A good nut from him takes discipline
but done the right way I was sure I could make him bust just
the way he wanted to. Cesar grabbed the back of my head
and began fucking my mouth hard like he was fucking me in
the ass, a beating that I enjoyed on many other occasions as
well. This was sign number three and it was the one that
assured me that he would definitely not go limp or back out.
He was about to climax and it surprised me because it was a
little faster than usual. Then again I could do this all night

and never get tired so long as I relaxed my jaws.

"Fuck! I'm bout to cum!" He growled ramming into my mouth harder and faster.

I removed my hands from the equation bringing them around to his nice firm squeezable backside, aiding him in his pumping. My gag reflexes were calmer and nearly nonexistent since I had been doing this for so long. I tried to deep throat his cock every time he shoved it back inside. Cesar clenched my weave tightly as his muscles tensed up, flexing with every move he made.

"Open your fucking mouth." Cesar demanded.

I opened my mouth as wide as I could, preparing for him to shoot his shot. I smiled to remind him that I loved that type of shit. He looked down at my sex face knowing that he could cum all in my mouth and watch me play with it with my tongue. He jerked my head back like a rag doll as I stuck my tongue out leaving a landing strip for his seeds. He jerked back one final time and came back in full force grasping his piece in his hand, massaging the head as he skeeted all into my mouth, my eye, my nose, and my hair. He placed his tip into my mouth allowing me to suck the remaining flow from out of him. I opened my mouth wide, tilting my head back giving him proof that I swallowed it down with no problem.

"AH!" Cesar breathed as he fell back on the couch attempting to catch his breath.

"Mmm. How was that baby?" I asked seductively licking my lips.

"It was cool."

"Wha? Just cool huh?"

"Yeah. I mean you got a little toothy at the end but it did its job." He smirked getting up with his pants slopped around his legs headed to the bathroom.

"What? You ain't never had a problem before and the cum all over my face tells a different story too!"

"What do you want me to say, Mink? When you fucking them other niggas, you so wrapped up in their validations that you don't even see they don't give a fuck about you."

"I don't remember you complaining when the bills were coming up paid." I snapped crossing my arms, watching him undress and cut on the shower.

This nigga tried to front me off but he knew I wasn't

wrong. I may not have worked a real job but I sure held it down when he couldn't, not to mention put money in his pocket and gas in the truck on his broke days. I know he didn't think I was really borrowing that much money from my momma, did he? Cesar knew me better than that. He knew I would never ever go ask my momma for anything other than her love especially if I didn't have to. I hated asking her for shit because when I first left her house at seventeen, I vowed that I would never again need or ask her for anything. Since then I've stayed true to my word and he knew that.

"Man, I hope it was worth it." Cesar spat trying to close the bathroom door on me.

"Wait," I said halting the door from its swing. "What the fuck does that mean?"

"It means whatever you want it to mean, Mink. It's your world baby girl. I'm just a squirrel getting a nut." Cesar snarled as he slammed the door smack dab in my face securing the lock behind it.

Chapter 5— Cesar

Shitted, showered, and shaved, I exited the bathroom feeling food as the air brushed against my wet skin sending a slight chill through my body and erecting my nipples. I snatched the big blue towel from the rack, wrapping it around my waist before pushing open the bedroom door. Mink was spread across the bed as thin as she was spreading that pussy, cackling away on the damn phone as usual. There was no telling who could be on the other end pumping her head full of hot air but shit, I really could care less.

"Hold on girl. Where you going?" Mink asked turning from her belly to her back, being nosey at what kind of clothes I was picking out of the closet.

"None of your damn business." I smirked. "Last time I checked, I was a grown ass man and my momma and daddy were dead."

"You ain't gotta be like that Cesar. I'm just saying, you didn't ask if I wanted to come."

I didn't know what kind of *come* she was talking about since she had just got through bussing me down but either way I wasn't feeling it, period. "Maybe I didn't ask you cause I didn't want you to go."

"But since CJ's gone and I thought we could catch up on some much needed time for us." She whined.

"Well you thought wrong cause I got plans." I smirked slipping my dark colored straight-legged Diesel jeans on over my blue plaid boxers.

I paired it with a black polo with matching color contempo sneaks, same brand. Looking at how sexy I looked in the large oval shaped dresser mirror, there was no doubt that I was feeling myself. I took a little Ocean Bath and Body Works aftershave from the dresser and dabbed the fresh scent onto my face and neck. The musk wasn't complete until I sprayed the body spray on my chest and forearms to accentuate the crispness. After rolling some deodorant under my arms I was ready to hit the streets. I could feel Mink's eyes pierce through the back of my head like a laser beam as I walked out the bedroom door headed to the living room in search of my keys and wallet.

"It's her...isn't it?" Mink asked in a light tone. "You getting all snazzy for her?"

"See, there you go trippin' again. Can't a man just go out in peace without you clockin' him all the damn time? Shit you party enough for the both of us and you got the nerve to be worried about what I'm doing." I couldn't help but laugh at her ass.

"But...I mean what time will you be back?"

"There you go again." I smirked picking up my keys and wallet off of the floor as I moved towards the front door.

"Cesar..."

"Bye Mink."

"Cesar, wait! Cesar!"

She could call my name all she wanted but I was gone on her ass. She wasn't about to ruin my night with her bullshit. I loaded into the truck and headed down the street. My fingers toggled quickly through the contacts in my phone pressing send when I reached the name of the person I needed to reach.

"What's good, killa?"

"Nothing much. 'Bout to slide through. Where you at?" I replied.

"At Passion."

"That's what I thought. I'll be there in about fifteen." I said before hanging up the phone.

It had been a while since I went out to do anything seeing as though I was always working like a slave to make the chump change for my family. I never really had time to do shit and when I did all I wanted to do was sleep. At the end of the day, I didn't give a fuck. My family was eating and my boy needed for nothing, that's all I cared about. My feelings didn't matter, nor did my pain or happiness. Nothing mattered before them, not even life.

I pulled up in front of Passion a short while later parking the truck in the oversized parking lot. It was 10pm on the dot, still early as hell according to the party scene. The night was still young for some of these thirsty niggas trying to score some ass and these females trying to come up on their next balling baby daddies. Shit if I had known any better when I was younger I wouldn't have even fucked with Mink's young ass and would've just got me a plethora of hoes to wet my dick. But my dumbass had to go and try to turn a hoe into a housewife.

"What up, Cesar?" The bouncer June greeted me flexin' his big ass biceps like he was scaring somebody.

"Aye boi, put them guns away with your ball headed ass. You ain't scaring nobody over here." We chuckled as I walked past him and the long line of waiting patrons, heading towards the door.

Passions was one of Yolo's many businesses across Chicago, located just outside of the Forest Park suburb, this one was his favorite. He loved the suburbs feeling that businesses would be more lucrative out there, but the city was my home. It was the one Flava least likely frequented and where he could let his hair down and fuck with a few bussers if he wanted to. See the nigga did his dirt but he did it smooth. Flava never had to worry about no chickens calling her phone harassing her and he always put her on the pedestal she deserved to be on. He never let another disrespect her and for that she never tripped on him about where he was or how late he was out. As long as I've known him I've never even heard him complain about her blowing up his phone buggin' about dumb shit. She was classy and knew her place which was right next to his throne; some shit I wished I had.

Every six months this fool changed the color of the club and for these six months the theme was red. I actually liked the way the club was set up with the booths in the far corner for business purposes and the tables on the other side of the dance floor where the regulars couldn't bother them. The stairs to the VIP separated them from the dance floor as well leaving it rather dark in that corner with about five half-moon shaped plush red sofa and table sets. The full glass bar was to my right, all lit up with bright red lighting; making sure that the hundreds of booty shakers could see it and make their way over there to spend some dough. It was popping tonight too. It was still early and it looked like people was already drunk as hell dancing on the floor.

This place was huge, even though from the outside it almost looked like it was nonexistent; if it weren't for the big ass pink Passions sign out there it probably would be. I made my way through the musty and sweaty crowd; back to the booths where I found Yolo and two of his dudes. They were hugged up on some raggedy looking females while Yo was on the phone looking too serious. It amazed me that this fool could hear anything with Meek Mill and Rick Ross blaring through speakers from the corners of the ceilings as the DJ banged his head hard in his booth thinking and chanting that he was A Boss.

"Aye, Yo. Whaddup?" I said walking up to the table as his goons eyed me from head to toe with raised eyebrows.

"Whaddup nigga? I see you came out boi boi!" Yolo
replied calming his goons down when they saw that he knew
me as we shook up. He finished up his call immediately. "Hit
me back when you know something nigga and not a minute
later."

His goons moved out of the way giving him ample
space to get up from his seat as the strobe lights danced
throughout the room. Yolo smiled as he grabbed the back of
my neck roughly pulling me towards the winding staircase. I
followed him up the stairs and past three VIP Passion Rooms
to his king-size glass paned office. He looked down on all of
the people juking in his establishment, never even cracking a
smile.

"You know how much money I make a night in this
club alone, Cesar?" Yolo asked firing up a fat ass cigar.

"Naw, shit. But um, since we're on the subject of
money—"

"You know these niggas that run up behind me every
day, all day, are nothing but yes men. I don't need yes men
in my crew. I'm thinking about axing all their asses. Ya
know?"

"Yeah...yeah..."

"I'm saying them niggas ain't loyal. I wanna revamp my whole operation. Ya feelin' me C-Note?" Yolo spoke turning to face me as he lowered his cigar.

"Yeah, I feel you Yo." The look of shock read on my face cause no one had called me C-Note since my gang bangin' days. Obviously this nigga had done his homework on me.

"So, I know you a family man and shit, you gone on the straight and narrow. I can respect that." He said lifting his cigar up to his lips, pointing it slightly my way. "But I know what you capable of. I know what your real potential is and it ain't working no whack ass job for scraps."

At that moment it felt like he was insulting me and praising me at the same damn time. I didn't know whether or not to say fuck him or thank him for his remarks. Instead I remained silent. In this game, silence was golden. It was worth more than thirty bars of gold and I knew how to be a man of few words. Yolo pulled his beaded braids from out of the back of his shirt letting them fall to his back then took a seat extending his hand to offer me one.

"Yolo, I really didn't want to do this but I feel like with my background ain't nobody gon' hire me man. Then Mink fucked my paperwork up." I couldn't do anything but lower my head in disgust.

"Aye," Yolo began in his second culture's accent, Spanish. "That's my wife's sister and all, but that bitch is a hoe. Straight up. She gots to go. I don't know how you gonna do it but that bitch is nothing but trouble. Ya feel me?"

"Yeah, I feel you. I already know."

"Okay, you handle that shit. Anyway ain't nothing wrong with what I do, vatho. I make good dough and have been for years. These cops get their cut and that's how we're able to operate the way we want to. Everybody got their hands out but they're like dogs graveling at my fucking feet. Those are the niggas you feed the scraps too."

"Aight, Yo. So what you want me to do?" I asked hesitantly, replanting my feet firmly on the ground.

"I don't need anything from you bro. But I figure you could help yourself by coming aboard the team and becoming what you were born to be."

I couldn't deny that I knew exactly what he was talking about. I swear that was a job that I thought I'd never have to do again. It wasn't all bad but it was the getting caught shit that made me want to quit in the first place. Dismembering bodies while they were still alive and torturing information out of them just to get a one up on the competition was on the agenda and I knew it. I never had trouble sleeping when I did that shit back in the day, and all I had to do was reposition my thoughts inside of my hard exterior so that I felt nothing once more.

"Man, I ain't trying to do no cleaning work, Yo." I replied wondering if I could get out of doing any dirty work under his hand.

"You will once I tell you that it's not the type of cleaning you're used to." When he spat that a sense of relief covered my entire body.

"Word?"

"I want you to take my motherfucking business to the next level. I want you to get rid of these clowns for me and find some real worthy, loyal, and trustworthy niggas that never crack a smile and are all about business." Yolo spat rising from his seat to meet me in front of the desk. "So what do you say? You ready to make some real bread?"

"Shit...you laying a lot on a nigga all at once. I just wanted to do this long enough to get some bread to save or maybe open my own business so I ain't gotta fucks with no petty jobs like that. What you're talking is some long term shit, Yo."

"Nigga, I'm thinking long term. I've been knee deep in this shit for 15 years and I've lasted this long only because I've had real niggas in my corner. But everybody has to go sometime right? I'm just giving you an opportunity to get on. If you stay you stay, but if you go…know there is no coming back." Yolo said placing his cigar in the ashtray.

I sat there stroking my chin wondering what this fool's angle was. I mean I knew the cat, but I didn't really know the cat, never really studied him the way I needed to since I was never really around him. The squinting of his eyes told me that he was all about his business and wasn't playing any games. It seemed like now or never to give him an answer that this opportunity would not be extended to me again. All that kept replaying over and over again in my head was my son's voice asking me for something that I couldn't provide.

"Whew," I exhaled slowly and reluctantly answered. "alright dude. When do you need me to start?"

"Awe shit, C-Note's back in the game!" Yolo smirked, making one single clap loudly.

"Naw. C-Note is dead dude. It's just Cesar now."

"Oh, I feel you! You on some ol' grown man shit. Well that's wassup fool."

"Yeah, yeah. So what do you need me to do first?" I asked standing to look down out of the window at the crowd.

"You're at the right place at the right time. You see those fools down there. That one's Drake and that there is Mo. Now both of those motherfuckas head the trap house over on 65th and Whipple, you know the one. But I believe that either one or both of them fools have been trickin' and dippin'. I need you to be my second set of eyes out there you feel me." Yolo said placing his hand firmly on my shoulder.

"Yeah I feel you."

"Whoever it is, Cesar, I don't give a fuck. Let me know so I can get rid of the son of bitch. You understand? But it's up to you to build me a trustworthy trap. Meet them motherfuckas over there at 6am to setup. You heard me?"

"Yeah, yeah. I got you."

"Cesar, this is your baby now. They'll be rewards if you make me proud C. Don't fail me and don't cross me. Disloyal ass niggas take dirt naps. Ya feel me?"

I didn't take too kindly to threats but I knew he was just trying to get me to understand that he meant business and that this shit was nothing personal. I would have to prove myself worthy of his trust just like the next motherfucka and there would be no favoritism or slack cut upon me just because I was kind of like family to him. I couldn't expect it any other way. I knew what the game was like and this was my choice to jump back in it. Yeah the players change but the game was still the same. I stared blankly out the window feeling crazy that I had found myself back in some shit like this. Feeling like if I failed this and went to jail that I would not only fail myself and the seven years I spent getting my life back on track but I would also fail my son, who was looking up to me and watching everything I did.

"Yeah, Yolo. I feel you dude." I said gazing down at the dancers noticing a shiny silvery dress swaying its thick thighs through the crowd.

Yolo slammed the half-filled bottle of Jack down on the desk after pouring two carefully filled shots. Even though my attention was elsewhere I kept my focus on him. I was only back in the game for a split second and already my skills had kicked right back into high gear. Only trust who you need to, not one more. I took the shot from him toasting it to the air keeping my eyes locked on his. He was no fool his self and knew how to play it. I was cool with that; cause proving myself was something I was no stranger to.

"Welcome back to the underworld, dog." Yolo recited before his cheeks curled in shining a smile so bright it could blind.

I didn't even think to thank him nor did a smile wipe across my face. I wasn't happy about my decision to enter the ranks again but real men make sure their family eats, no matter what. Still my attention flourished around the silver dress feeling as if I had seen her from somewhere before. The spotlight crept across her face quickly and within that brief second I caught a glimpse of who she was.

"Aye, Yo. I'll holla at you tomorrow." I said patting him on the back and heading towards the door.

"Hold fast. Where you going, man?"

"I need to holla at somebody right quick. I got you though, in the morning." My feet couldn't move faster out of the door and down the stairs to the dance floor.

My eyes skimmed through the crowd for the unique sparkling dress but the harder I looked the more the job became like finding a needle in a haystack. Quickly my hopes died, lowering my searching eyes to the floor. She was gone in an instant and it pissed me off to the max. I was amazed that she had gotten out of the packed club scene that quickly, like a ninja. I gave up, reaching in my pocket for my car keys figuring I'd head to the crib and get some sleep before the spot in the morning when I felt this light tapping on my shoulder.

"Hey Cesar." Her voice sounded sweetly from behind me.

"Hey...Lasha." I smiled giving her a playful pinch on the chin. "I didn't know you liked to come here."

"Yeah well, there are a ton of things you didn't know about me." She said sipping from the skinny black straw of her orange colored drink.

"Well, maybe we need to do something about that." I replied taking her drink from her and setting it on the bar. I didn't want her lit up while we got to know each other better. "Wanna go somewhere and talk?"

"You know I do." She said placing her soft well manicured hand in mine.

Chapter 6— Mink

"Girl this motherfucka been gone for two hours now. I bet you he with that trick ass, Lasha. I swear when I catch that bitch, that ass is through." I snapped popping my gum with my teeth.

"Now Mink you know your scary ass ain't gonna do shit." Flava snickered through the phone.

"Dang Flav, why you always gotta trip on me like that? You don't know what I'm gonna do. That man belongs to me, okay? As long as I got his son, that fool ain't going anywhere. Shit, I'll be damned if I lose my meal ticket." I replied.

"Girl you trippin'. You don't even know what he's doing. He's probably out with Yolo makin' money."

"Flava, the man gets heated every time I ask him to go to Yolo. I know for a fact, he ain't with Yolo. He's got to be with that trick. Look could you call him on three way one more time and see if he answers your phone?"

"Mink, I'm tired of playing hood rat games with you. I don't police Yolo because I trust him. Even when I don't wanna trust him, I trust him."

"Why?" My lip curled in disgust.

"Cause that's what real women do, Mink. They stand by their man." She recited as if she was spitting something so deep.

"Stand by your man, yeah. But mine is broke. Why should I stand by his ass?"

"I'm too over you, Mink. Call me back after you've slept your ignorance off. Good night." Flava exhaled as she hung up the phone in my ear.

Livid, I just wanted to call her back and snap on her but I knew my anger was misdirected. There were no words that could express how paranoid I actually was that he was out there in the middle of the night with some skank that had nothing on me. I mean she was shorter and lighter skinned almost to the point of being white but she still had nothing on me. Every nigga was hypnotized by my thick ass thighs and mocha flavored honey.

I reached into my panty drawer pulling out an old emergency pack of Newport 100's that I only smoked one cigarette a day out of. It was my way to quit smoking just not all at once, cold turkey. Considering my life was beginning to fall apart right before my eyes, a cig was just right for the occasion. This nigga was out there cheating on me just as I did him but the only difference was, I ain't letting his ass go without a fight. He could sleep with a thousand bitches but his dick and his money will forever belong to me. I stamped that shit when that five pound eight ounce seed busted through my uterus. Damn, my phone's ringing again. This had better be him.

"Hello?"

"Yeah baby what up? This Cash."

"Cash? From where?"

"Com' on now Mink, quit playin'. That nigga that was munchin' on that pretty ass pussy that day your man tried to whoop that ass. You remember that don't you?"

"Oh...Hey Cash." I smirked having fun teasing his sexy sounding ass. "I'm just fucking with you boy. What's up?"

Cash was a short, stocky 5'6" dark skinned nigga that I had met at the club one night a few weeks back. He was a cutie and was slick with the tongue verbally and physically.

But he always talked about cuffing a bitch, which was something he knew I wasn't on. Still, I couldn't resist being around him. He dressed like he was fresh out of a Ebony magazine and he carried his self so highly like he was mingling with red carpet celebrities and shit. I wanted that life. Not to mention that he spoiled me buying me whatever I wanted.

"I need you to look around your room and check for my wallet. I think I left it there the other night when your nigga tried to bust a cap in my ass."

"Um...I haven't seen no wallet, Cash." I said rising up from the bed, giving the room a once over again.

"It should've been by your bed. Can you check again cause I need that shit for my job?" Cash sniffed sternly.

"Uh huh and what is it that you do again?"

"I'm an executive at the headquarters for a national company." He chuckled.

I knew he was beating around the bush not really wanting to tell me exactly what he did for a living but it didn't matter cause when I picked up his wallet from under the bed and searched through it, I already had my answer.

"Nope, sorry. Nothing's in here Cash. But I'll be sure to keep you posted if it happens to surface." I lied nearly hanging up on him.

If he wanted it back he would have to go through my man's Glock to get it and I knew for a fact that wasn't going to happen. I pulled out one of the ten credit cards that were neatly tucked down inside the dark brown foldable wallet. The nice platinum Visa would do. All I could think about was all the shit I could buy with them. My hand was itching like crazy, wishing the mall was open right now so I could go and get me another bag from Macy's.

That nigga was crazy if he thought I was going to give him anything back. In the dresser mirror, I took a look at my weave realizing that it needed a little touching up and decided it was time to go see Gigi. That fool could lay some butters and he was the only one me and Flava allowed in our heads. Period. My fingers couldn't dial his number fast enough as I stuck the wallet and the cards deep behind my colorful array of panties and bras.

"Bitch, I'm coming over tomorrow. I need a touch up." I said as Gigi answered the phone, checking the front door for opening noises.

"What? Wait who is this? Mink?" He smacked in his

cute flamboyant way. "Oh no bitch I'm not fucking with you on that level at gunpoint unless you got the scratch you owe me from the last few times. You heard me?"

"Quit poppin' off. I'm gonna get your little change to you. Now put me on the books for early in the morning. I got some things I need to do and I don't wanna have to wait."

"Excuse you miss thing, come calling me like you in high demand or something boo boo. You'll get fit in when you get fit in. How about that?"

"Gi, why are you playing me?"

"Uh, cause you're cheap, honey. Yes, you." He smacked his lips in disgust.

I had been playing him these past few weeks but it was only because he let me. Shit, just because he was gay didn't mean he didn't still think and feel like a man. It never goes away no matter how much booty you like to bust and because of that reason he got played like the rest of them. I couldn't help it. I needed my hair did and Cesar kept telling me to wait and my dip offs were all playing me so I had to do what I had to do.

Yeah, me and Gi have been friends since Freshman year of high school and we've always had each other's backs.

He was this skinny little flamboyant dude with psychedelic hairstyles, fresh gear, and sassy ways and I was the party chick who never liked to hang with the "in-crowd". Through thick and thin we stuck together but he should've known better than to trust all this thickness. At the end of the day, ass was ass and when I rubbed this big ol' thang up against his growing beast he could never resist it.

"I said I got you bitch. Now quit playing." I retorted sick of the back and forth action he was sending.

"Alright now. Don't get here and don't have my money cause we gon' have it out."

"Awe shut up nigga you ain't gon' do nothing but whip that big ass monster out again and bust this ass wide open like you like to do, boo." My laughter grew hysterical.

"Okay that was lovely but that only bought you time. You still gotta run me my money so boop boop. Jokes on you." He laughed harder than I did. "Butt is fun for the nut but money pays the bills."

His enjoyment pissed me off a little but I let him have his fun for the moment. After all, the dude could smoke some hair. My ears damn near went deaf listening to him rant and rave about how loose my pussy was and that niggas were lined up with one dollar bills in hand just to get a taste. We've joked like that for years but it wasn't until today that it began to hurt my feelings coming from him. I held the phone slightly away from my head in an attempt to drown him out as I walked to the kitchen to get a bottle of ice cold water from the frig. The front door knob jiggled a bit, making me think someone was trying to get in after noticing all of the lights off in the living room. I panicked for a second searching the knife block on the counter for the longest, deadliest, sharpest one on in the pack.

"Gigi, save that shit. I gotta call you back cause somebody's trying to break up in here." I whispered hanging up while he was in midsentence.

"It better be Publisher's Clearinghouse with a big ass check or it's on!" I yelled snatching the longest butcher knife from the block standing on the side of the island that sectioned off the kitchen from the living room.

My eyes glanced over to the microwave checking for the time, 3:45am, as the door finally swung open.

"You standing there like you gon' do something. What the fuck you gon' do, girl? Nothing with your scary ass." Cesar snorted and laughed stumbling a bit inside before slamming the door.

"Nigga don't slam that door. You'll wake the neighbors and that's all we need is to get put out of this motherfucka." I said sliding the knife back in the block as he stumbled to the back bedroom.

"Don't you ever just shut the fuck up sometimes?" Cesar said flopping down on the bed right on his belly hard as ever.

I hadn't seen him this intoxicated in a long time. As a matter of fact the last time he was wasted like this was when we conceived CJ. A smile grew upon my face. I couldn't help it as the thoughts raised in my mind of how to get this nigga back on track. I could guilt him so quickly into taking the job with Yolo I'd be sitting rich and pretty in a matter of weeks. The one thing that I knew would motivate him, unfortunately another baby.

"You want me to rub your feet, baby?" I asked through his groans and grunts.

He was out of it so badly that he couldn't even speak. It was a shock to me that he had made it home but he was always good with shit like that. I removed his shoes; his elongated feet hung over the bed letting them tumble onto the floor carelessly. Cesar began to snore heavily like a bear hit with a tranquilizer dart burying his face in the pillow he was snuggled with. It was like moving a log but with a few shoves I was able to force him over onto his back in order to remove his shirt and pants. His body jerked a little before releasing a mild cough, stirring as if he were trying to wake up.

"Just relax daddy. Momma's gonna make you feel all better." I whispered in the most sensual voice possible.

The ripples of muscle mass on his chest felt so good under my hands as I rubbed his chest, caressing the sexiness of him. I saw his dick jump repeatedly as if to indicate that my mini-massage felt just as good to him. My tongue made its way from his brown nipples moving simultaneously between the two on down to the crease in between his thigh and his torso. I sucked gently on his skin watching him jerk and tense up from the jolt of excitement his body was being riddled with.

I could hear the faint sounds of deep moaning coming from his masculine lips. He licked and bit them trying his hardest not to scream out in ecstasy but his movements were enough to let me know what he felt. No words were needed. As I moved down to his now rock hard dick standing straight up at attention, I couldn't help but notice that at its hardest it looked like it had grown longer since the last time I saw it. He must've been really horny for his dick to be that damn hard. Slapping my mouth onto it, I slurped and bobbed as fast as I could, interlocking my fingers around it moving up and down as my head did.

Cesar covered his eyes with his arm breathing heavily and curling his toes. I pummeled his dick swallowing, choking just like he was used to. He loved that shit. It was how I always got my way with him. Just as his mouth was about to release a torrent of intoxicatingly sexual moans, I jumped up quickly stripping my body of all my unwanted clothes then mounted him before he had a chance to rethink my advances.

"Ooo, shit!" He whispered still biting his lip.

He hated when I jumped off of him abruptly like that but I had something better planned for him. I crawled my naked body on top of his; titties dangling in limbo. I then straddled him, adjusting my wet pussy to align with his swollen eight-inch dick. I rotated my hips in a way to allow his manhood to slide right on in me. I began to ride my stallion. As I moved up and down slowly, I could feel my juices gently coat his shaft and the sensation of it now deep inside of me; knocking on my uterus' door! There was slight pain but oh so much pleasure as he rubbed against my walls sending tingling sensations through my soul. I could feel him jerk inside of me trying to hold his cum, so he didn't bust too fast.

"You wanna cum in your pussy baby?" I growled at him. "Huh?"

Cesar didn't speak. He usually loved to talk dirty in bed but I guess either he was too inebriated for that or he locked in total sex face, he was still mad at me. I didn't care. I bounced harder, bringing my ass all the way up to the tip of his dick and slapping it all the way down; my pussy swallowing it whole, taking that dick like a true champ. I did it again slapping down on his waist harder and harder showing him that only real women like me took the dick that well and he would never find another bitch like me.

He pulled himself up on his elbows, nudging his head in my direction giving the signal for me to lean in so he could suck on my pretty ass brown nipples. It was like he couldn't wait for me to lean in, devouring my nipples like he was sucking for milk. That shit felt so good and had my pussy throbbing heavy; feeling like I wanted to cum. I locked my walls tight around his shaft, bouncing faster and faster as Cesar wrapped his strong muscular arms around my waist; resting just above my ass. He tensed his waist to halt his bouncing as much as he could, locking me in so he could shove his dick harder inside of me.

"ARGH!" I shrieked wrapping my arms around his neck praying for sweet relief.

There was no way I was going to beg for him to stop though. I could feel the pain escalate in the pit of my stomach as he stabbed his dick deeper and deeper inside of me. Tears streamed down my face gradually as I leaned my head on his shoulder, praying for him to cum soon. He gripped my back side, fucking me harder and harder and there was nothing I could do other than sit there and take it. My baby was going to get all of this pussy even if it killed me cause in the end I only wanted one thing.

"UGH!" He bellowed slamming me down hard; holding me still, a smile crept across my face.

Cesar strong-armed me, grabbing my waist trying to throw me off of him. I already knew what time it was. He was spewing all of that lovely, thick and creamy goodness inside of me. *It's okay baby, I got this.* I released all of my weight onto his legs, feeling them tremble in their weakness. He released a torrent of groans before freeing his strong grip of my midsection and flopping back on the bed in exhaustion. There was nothing he could do; I had it all inside of me now. Quickly I wiped my smile away before he could detect my happiness in the darkness as I rose from his now half limp half hard shaft. My baby was like that, always ready at the drop of a dime.

"What you do that shit for, Mink?" He breathed as I hopped off his lap.

"What shit baby? I was just merely in the moment. You know how good that daddy dick be feeling to me baby." I secretly smirked as I nearly limped off to the bathroom.

"We agreed we weren't going to have no more kids right now." He yelled as I turned the hot water on the faucet pretending not to hear him. "We agreed dammit!"

"Huh? Hold on, I can't hear you babe." I yelled back smirking hard as ever now, taking my face towel from the rack dipping it under the running water.

"I said I thought we agreed!"

"Ah!" I screamed. "What you doing sneaking up on me like that? You scared the shit out of me."

"Maybe somebody needs to so you can stop doing stupid shit, Mink."

"Stupid shit? Nigga, you trippin' for real. We got one

baby together already. What does it matter if we have another one?"

"It matters cause we don't need no more kids right now! We can barely take care of the son we got, why the fuck would we bring another mouth to feed in the picture?"

"Baby, we're gonna be fine. I got faith in you as a man. You gonna do what you gotta do to keep us straight." I said caressing the side of his cheek.

"Naw, you ain't getting this shit, Mink!" Cesar said backing up hastily from my grasp. "I don't want no more kids by your ass!"

"Wha...huh?"

"You heard me, right. I ain't got time to start this clock all over again with you. CJ is almost grown and after that I never have to deal with your ass again." Cesar said storming his naked body into the kitchen, dick swinging and all. Even with a limp dick that man could swing. I gently bit my lip.

"What are you saying, Cesar? Are you trying to say you wanna break up with me?" My heart beat a mile a minute feeling like this time was much more different than all the rest of times he had threatened it was over.

"I'm saying, anything not regarding my son I don't give a fuck about. We're done here, Mink." He said grabbing the bag of green seedless grapes out of the fridge before heading back towards the bedroom. "You can sleep on the couch."

"Agh!" I gasped feeling as if the wind had been knocked up out of me as he slammed our bedroom door, mildly hyperventilating.

Chapter 7— Cesar— The Next Morning

I arrived at the spot about fifteen minutes early making sure I posted up in the cut to see how these kats entered the joint on a daily basis. I wanted to see how they started the day-to-day operation before I jumped right into it, wrecking their shop and bringing order to what Yolo described as chaos. My head turned down at the blunt I was rolling and just as I looked up, two dudes walked up to open the door to the nearly rundown bungalow, looking around all suspicious like. If the cops were watching their asses they sure as hell looked suspect and obvious like they were looking to get caught on some dumb shit. The sun was shining down bright as hell on these two dark skinned dudes as they struggled to open the door to the house like they were doing it for the first time.

My blunt finally pearled, I sparked it taking a few quick puffs before putting it out and setting it in my ashtray. My mind was mellow as I released my Glock from the glove compartment and exited the car, stuffing it behind my back in my jeans. I was ready to put the shock value into them dudes, because I knew they weren't expecting me. I walked up to the house checking out the yard noticing that there were two cameras hidden in each bush and as I walked up the stairs to the porch there were two more at each end of the house pointing towards the door. All that was cool and everything but they didn't even appear to be working. If I wasn't mistaken, they were the motion sensor ones that moved with body movement but they didn't follow me anywhere.

I peered in the window checking to see what these dudes were on and checking for their specific location in the house. These dudes were in the house on some raggedy ass couch laid back like they were trying to catch some fucking z's. Clearly they were costing Yolo money which would in turn cost me money now and that was some shit I wasn't having, not period.

"Aye yo, who is it?" One of the niggas barked as I banged roughly on the door like I was the police.

"Cesar."

"Who?"

"Yolo's brother in law, man. Open the fucking door." I bellowed keeping my eyes on the corner where traffic turns onto the block.

"Aye man he ain't tell us nobody was comin' up in here." The dude said as he flung open the door scratching at the long ass scar running from the middle of his chest all the way down his belly.

"Well call him if you need verification of my presence but I'm about to tell you that I'm in this piece now." I replied walking in observing the substandard living conditions these niggas were squandering in.

"I'm about to buzz that nigga right now." Dude said as he reached into his jeans angrily for his cell. "And for your sake it better not be no bullshit."

"Man, y'all niggas know who I am. Wake the fuck up, up in here. You motherfuckas have obviously been sleeping up in here too long." I yelled waking the dude up who was passed out on the beat up old gray three-cushioned couch.

This joint looked like it had been a previous crime scene that was never cleaned. There was garbage everywhere in the large living room, making it look small from all the piles of clothes and trash coupled with the stench of forty dead men. I turned, looking around the corner into the small empty dirty kitchen; watching as a swarm of dark brown roaches nestled on the white double sink making the faucet their stomping ground. I hated anything that crept or crawled across anything but I manned it up, rolling my eyes back towards the sorry ass motherfucka looking mad as hell, pressing the phone firmly to the side of his head.

"Yeah, Yo." The dude said as he hung up the phone.

"So, I'm sure he's verified why I've made my presence known." I smirked knowing the thought was burning him to his very core.

"I'm Drake and that's Mo. We run this motherfucka, aight? So anything you do or take goes through us first. You got that, bro in law?" Drake snarled stepping closer into the sunlight shining through the front window.

He was young in the face, they both were, couldn't have been more than eighteen or nineteen. It suddenly dawned on me why this nigga wasn't making any money up in here. Because he had two young, dumb, lazy asses up in here running things since he was too lazy to do it himself. I knew Yolo couldn't have ever stopped in to check on his operation because there was no way in hell he would allow these fools to lounge up in here like this without making any money. Shit just didn't seem right up in here.

"I'm sorry to bust your shit playboy. But I don't take

orders from scab ass niggas like you. I give 'em. So if you ain't here to make no money then you need to take your ass back to wherever the fuck you came from. Cause we about our dough up in here." I snarled letting these niggas know I meant business.

Mo rose from the couch looking at his boy as if to give the eye that they each wanted to try me. It was cool; I was ready for them too. These niggas didn't know me or anything about me. They didn't know that while I was in jail, all I did was fight niggas to keep their asses in check and let them know I was no punk. They didn't know that I benched two seventy five and that was on a bad day. Mo's nappy matted hair looked like a wasps nest standing on top of his head as he raised his hand to scratch it before walking over to Drake.

"Com' on man let's just get this shit over with so we can bounce." Mo said slapping the back of his hand against Drake's bare chest.

"Yeah, aight. But fuck all that giving orders shit like you running anything other than your mouth. I'm in and out this bitch you feel me." Drake spat as he rolled his eyes dragging a stool from the dirty ass kitchen to the front door.

"Y'all got white all tightened up?" I asked searching

the room for product.

"Yeah man, it's in the flue." Mo responded emerging from the kitchen with a struggle sandwich, which was nothing more than thick ass government bologna and dry bread.

"Well how much is in there, motherfucka? We're about to be open for business in thirty fucking minutes and you niggas ain't got shit set up over here." I snapped checking my cell for the time, 6:35am.

"Chill nigga, damn. We run this." Drake laughed.

"Yeah, we don't get that much business at this spot no way." Mo added.

"This is Marquette Park, a prime location and it should be poppin'. Y'all fuckin' up taking money out of Yolo's pocket and when you take from him you take from me and I don't lose money for shit. Ya feel me?"

They side eyed me to stare at each other before chuckling silently with their heads down. I didn't know what the joke was about and I didn't care. All I knew was that if they kept fucking around they would soon be the joke. I could see my demands for them to produce the product were falling on deaf ears.

"Dude, I don't think you heard me the first time and I don't like to repeat myself. Just get the fucking merch man." I retorted calmly.

Drake threw the forks up to Mo signaling for him to dig the product out from flue of the chimney. I could tell that Mo was like the bitch of their relationship and he would less likely give me as much fever as Drake would. The wooden porch began to rumble letting me know what time it was, but those fiends would have to wait. This shit needed to go as smoothly as possible and if that meant those thirsty suckas out there would be late getting their fixes, then so be it. Drake and Mo needed to be briefed on the ins and outs of how to run a real business.

Mo finally got the product out and brought it to the filthy, old food ridden, roach egg infested small cocktail table leaning against the wall, slapping a large Ziploc bag full of work down on top of it. I tried not to let the filth around me affect the task at hand, swallowing my spit before allowing vomit to follow it out of my mouth and onto the floor.

"Aight, check it. Everything is gonna run in an assembly line right at the door. That way shit moves quicker. Mo you sit your ass at the door grabbing the money and Drake will distribute. You need to listen to what the clucker has to say because they only gonna say a few words before they move on. Motherfuckas ain't got time to pussy foot around. Mo you fill this shoe box with the dough, make sure it's all there before you drop it in there, but I'm sure you won't have to worry. These fools don't wanna die today." I recited feeling much more like I did years ago when I was running my own shit, like the king.

"Yeah and while we're working, what'chu gonna do, man?" Drake barked looking back at me.

"The best job of all playboy, security. I'm gonna make sure that for two hours you don't get your ass popped off." I grinned, feeling the anger rise in the room.

The blood boiled inside of Mo for a small second before he returned to his normal aloof like state. Drake, on the other hand, turned around steadfast on his stool looking like he had just taken an ugly shit in the bathroom. I started to ask him what the hell his problem was, but knowing that I had pissed him off multiple times within the hour I had been here was satisfactory and I couldn't ruin that.

"Open the door." I instructed.

"Maannn…" Drake mumbled under his breath while rolling his eyes.

"You think I give a fuck about your attitude, lil' nigga. If you don't like it then quit." I calmly replied. "Now it's 7:01 am. Open the fuckin' doors, goofy."

I stood at the door, gawky squinted eyed as business flowed like clockwork. It staggered in the beginning but once word got out that we were supplying that good at fair prices the herd flocked to the crib. Business was good for my first day but it could've been better and as we shut down the trap at 9am on the dot I knew exactly what to expect at 8pm that night. The word would have flourished and we would have made a name for ourselves in that short time. Yolo had good product it's just that no one knew about it because these lame ass niggas weren't advertising it for sale. I squared them both off and noticed their jumpy demeanors; the entire amount of product was gone and I had a shoebox full of cash to take back to Yo. Their hands were itching like the skin of some of those dope fiends they just sold to. I side eyed their asses as I shook my head; without saying anything to them, I scooped up the box and headed for the truck. I had some info for Yolo and it wasn't going to be nothing nice.

Chapter 8- Mink

"Man, when you gon' drop that nigga and get wit a real man. You know I'm gon' take care of you girl." Cash said as my bra cupped my voluptuous tits while my fingers clinked the hooks together in the back.

"Cash now you know you ain't gon' take care of me the way I need to be and you know it so let's both quit playing ourselves. Okay?" I replied frantically looking for my beige tank top.

I was late for my hair appointment with Gigi and I knew he was going to be pitching a bitch as soon as I walked through the door. It was a good thing that Cash lived right around the corner from Yehia's in Hyde Park where Gigi worked. I really didn't feel like hearing his mouth but he would have to be all right at this point because when Cash called me talking about he was hungry again, I couldn't resist. Cash was a pussy eating connoisseur. This man did not like to eat pussy, he loved it, damn near craved it. Whenever he called me to tell me he was hungry my body would melt and my pussy would moisten. I needed that shit, especially as good as he was; he never skipped a beat, eating my pussy

for hours on end. In the beginning when I first met him at

the club, I thought I would die with him trying to suck every

bit of juice up out of me but after awhile of fucking him, it

started to become a necessity to me.

"Damn baby, you're always hitting me with that bull.

I'm a man of my word and if I say I'm gonna do something

then I'm gonna do it." He barked lying back on the bed

reaching his hand out to me.

"Yeah, okay, but what about my son?"

"What about him?"

"See, exactly my point. You don't like kids and I

come as a package deal, Cash."

"Shit, what the fuck that lil' nigga got to do with me?

As far as I'm concerned, that's that nigga's problem right?"

The words flew from his mouth raw and uncut and I

knew he meant them. That's all I needed was for Cesar to

have one hand up on me by having sole custody of our son

and he really wouldn't give me any fucking money then.

Naw, Cash was good for a good fuck but I would be a fool to

let him think he was going to trick me with that okie doke.

Before anything I'm a businesswoman and leaving Cesar

right now would definitely be bad for business.

"Anyway, since I couldn't find my damn wallet I canceled everything up in that bad boy." He grinned looking up at my face for a response. "So if you find my wallet just toss it in the trash. I'm good."

"Oh ok." I grimaced, rolling my eyes knowing that he had just fucked over my little come up.

"Yeah, so a nigga is never broke baby. You can gon' and move in with daddy." He chuckled.

"Would you shut the fuck up about that? Meanwhile I need some money. About two stacks should cover it." I said putting on my last flat shoe.

"Oh...oh I ain't got it. I mean I got it but it's in the bank." Cash grinned pulling me by the arm and back into the bed. "I know you didn't think I kept that kind of money on me."

"Ugh! Nigga I need that money like right now cause I got a hair appointment that I'm now late for."

"So. You women spend all day in the shop whether you got an appointment or not so what's the difference? Y'all be killing me." He smirked.

"Naw, you killing me cause you know the business and you still playing games."

"Yeah? No, playing games was having me come to your dude's house knowing there was a chance you could've gotten caught. And that nigga took you back huh?" Cash laughed.

"What's so funny? And no, he didn't take me back...we broke up."

"Word? All well shit you can get your shit and move on in then right?"

"No, Cash. Unless you gonna make room for CJ, I ain't doing nothing but fuck you and feed you. You got that?" I snapped trying to rise from his grasp.

He tossed me back on the bed pinning my arms down by my sides playfully. He sweetly and tenderly lined my neck with pecks from his soup cooler lips. His dark skin glistened in the morning rays shining through his small basement sized window. In fact, his entire apartment was small and it made wonder just how much money this nigga claimed he had. But it was a one-bedroom bachelor's pad and he was alone so I couldn't blame him for not wanting a lot of space.

"Cash, stop. I gotta go."

"Naw, you can get that shit did another day." He said as his stocky build mounted mine entirely reaching his hand down to stroke his manhood.

He wasn't as well-endowed as Cesar but what he was working with did do the job; when he worked it right. Lucky for him I was rocking my blue jean mini skirt, which gave him easy access to my plumped lip beauty. Just as he rolled my skirt up to my belly button my phone rang.

"Don't answer that shit." He mumbled through kisses.

"Hello?" I answered giving him the raised eyebrow as I hit the green call button on my touch screen.

"I know something you don't know."

"Now you know I hate it when you do that shit, Flav. Quit playing. What is it?"

"Ha ha ha."

"Flav what is it? I don't have time to play with you?" I was heated from that shit she did but my anger soon faded as Cash made his lips touch the ones in between my legs.

"Ugh fine. No fun having ass. Anyway, your man went to work for Yo this morning." Flava responded calmly.

"Oh my gosh! You're lying!"

"Would I waste my time calling you early as hell if I were? I don't know how many times I have to tell you that my time is money boo boo." She laughed.

I hated the way she spoke. So what she went to college and had a degree, she didn't have to talk to people like she was above them or something. If it weren't for the good news she was giving me, I would've cursed her ass out like I usually do. No, I didn't got to college to become some big shot but I refused to let her throw that or her degree in my damn face. I'm smart enough to make it and that's all I cared about. I wanted to jump up and call to curse Cesar out but I knew that would only ruffle his feathers more. Naw, this time I was going to sit back and play it cool and let him come to me.

"Thanks for the info sis. Good looking out." I said about to end the phone call. "See ya."

"You know the only way you're going to be able to hold on to that man is if you keep ya legs closed. I don't know where you went wrong, baby sis. We didn't raise you like this." Flava pressed on.

"Momma didn't raise me at all!"

"Damn, Mink, you're so fucking ungrateful. She was busy working two jobs trying to make a life for us." Flava snapped.

"Maybe if she hadn't have spread her legs to a worthless asshole she wouldn't have had to struggle with two bad ass kids." I retorted.

"Shit, speak for yourself. I wasn't as hot in the ass as you and I appreciate everything she's done for me. Mink you need to be a little bit more appreciative too."

"For what? So I can be a goody two shoes like you? Sorry everybody can't go to college and have our asses on our shoulders like you." I told her.

"Poor ungrateful spoiled brat had life so hard growing up in the fucking suburb of Oak Brook, where she went to great schools and played with the well-off white kids. You had the same opportunities I had, Mink. You just chose to go the lazy route."

"You know what fuck you, Flava! I don't have to listen to this shit."

"To what shit? The truth? Bitch you need a slap in the face and every time I try to give it to you, you run. Don't burn your bridge lil' sis."

"Are you done?" I asked heated from this entire call.

"No, just one more thing, sis. Don't be stupid all of your life. At some point you're gonna need to wake the fuck up."

I breathed, inhaling deeply before exhaling relief. Tears flowed from my eyes slowly trickling down the side of my cheeks as they closed unable to hold them open any longer. I was feeling some type of way, a sharp tingling sensation shot through my pelvis.

"Agh!" I exhaled.

"Bitch are you fucking while you on the phone with me?" The rise of Flava's voice let me know that I had succeeded in pissing her off.

"Sorry chick. It was out of my control." I giggled.

"Ugh, you're a nasty ass Mink, always thinking about yourself."

CLICK.

Ha. That bitch needed to be mad for a while. If she wasn't stuck on her high horse all the damn time maybe she could be like me. But all she knew to do was hate on me and be jealous. I didn't care what she or anyone else had to say about our relationship. In my eyes, she was nothing but another jealous hearted bitch.

"Now that you done came all in my mouth, let a nigga stick it in really quick." Cash said coming up from my snatch with wetness all around his lips.

"Mmm. I'd really love to but I've got to go. Sorry boo." I smiled as I jumped up straightening my clothes. "So how about that little scratch you owe me?"

"Owe you? You smokin' if you think I owe you something and anyway like I told you before, I don't have it on me. I'll bring it by tonight when I come and get you from the corner."

"What? Cash, don't fucking play with me." I snapped crossing my arms.

"Shut up girl you knew what I meant. I told you you're gonna meet me on the corner from now on cause I ain't going to that nigga's house and have him shoot my ass up."

"Scary ass." I mumbled. "You are really starting to piss me off. I ain't got time for this I gotta go."

Before he could respond, I walked out of the room and out of his house. Using him was easy as pie sometimes but he had those days when he made me work for it. I hated those days. Usually, I would oblige him but I had business to take care of. My cell exploded constantly with calls from Cash as I made my way around the corner to the shop. I didn't answer because I knew if I did he'd only want to fight. After pissing me off about my money already, I didn't have time to entertain that.

Three blocks later, I found myself at the doorstep of Yehia's Hair Shop on 53rd right off of Harper Street. The windows and the door were modest at best but once I stepped inside I felt like I was in hair Heaven. The smell of hair spray, shampoo and steam from the curling irons filled my nostrils almost making me want to do the happy dance. The walls were plain white as any other typical business; same for the floors, but what made this shop stand out from the rest were the twelve silver chairs and mirrors on each side of the shop. I could go to either one of those stylists and get my hair whipped to perfection, no problem, but I wanted Gigi. More like I needed him since I had no damn money.

"What's good baby?" I smiled sauntering to the back of the shop finding Gigi elbow deep in shampooing a client.

"Let me tell you something, boo boo. Okay, ain't nothing going on up in here if you ain't got my scrilla." He pointed flinging soap and water everywhere.

"Nigga I told you—"

"No, Mink! I need my cash front and center in my hand before I even touch that botched up shit you call a weave up there. And I can tell you ain't been takin' care of it neither." He frowned turning his big nose up at the sight.

"Gigi, I told you when I get the money I would pay you. Could you keep your voice down?" I whispered leaning in towards him.

"Well when you get that shit then I'll flip your whip other than that its desert storm up in this bitch!" He continued to yell looking down the way at his boss, who just so happened to be the owner and also his new beau.

"Ugh, I swear you get on my nerves." I mumbled angrily as I pouted and headed for the door.

"Hmm. Just like Flav gets on your nerves?" He asked watching my mouth drop open as I pivot pointed around on my heels.

"That heffa called you?"

"Mmhmm, and told me everything, honey. Word of advice, stop beating people up for telling you right; you were wrong, Mink.

"Ugh wrong my ass. How about having my back for change?" The sulking look on my face became impossible to hide.

"If you stay off of it long enough then maybe I will. Ha!" Gigi's words could have pierced through thick paned bulletproof glass right along with his hazel contacts followed suit.

Even if I wanted to ignore him I couldn't. He sashayed his skinny jean wearing, mocha skin having self through the shop. I was mad as ever but couldn't help but to admire his blonde faded Mohawk and the fact that he had been hitting the gym a little harder this week. As his bony arm swung effortlessly to shut and lock the door behind me, I couldn't help but wonder if I had indeed burned my bridge with him. I couldn't understand why none of my usual charm was working on him this time. On the way out the door and as it practically slammed behind me, I couldn't help but wonder if I was losing my touch. The rain that dripped onto my face as the thunder rolled on only confirmed my inner thoughts. For some reason, it was turning out to be one hell of a bad day. Regrettably, I took out my cell.

Yeah, it's C. You know what to do.

UGH! I know Cesar sees my fucking number. He's gotta be smokin' something to be treating me like this. Everybody was trippin' on me but it was all good because once I get on top they can all kiss my ass. I'm gonna make sure of that. Fuck them all. Desperate and hating the feeling that brought on, I gritted my teeth as I dialed another number into phone. It was a safety net that I knew by heart, one that would always do whatever I asked no matter what. I loved obedient niggas.

"Cash, can you take me home?" My lips cringed as my eyes lowered.

Chapter 9- Cesar – *4 weeks later*

"What's good girl?" I said putting the phone to my lips.

"Shit, you. You coming through?"

"I'm already in front of your building. Com' on and buzz me up."

"Dang, Cesar. That was quick. Here I come though." Her voice always sounded so sensual, so damn sexy.

Her super thick thighs danced down the stairwell as I watched through the long glass door, waiting for her to hit the lock. She wore red booty shorts with a white baby tee; both of which hugged her body so tightly they could have been painted on. I could not stop staring and even licked my lips a bit. She knew what she was doing and I knew what I wanted to do. The door opened and I walked in grabbing her, wrapping my arms around her soft body. The scent of sweet honey filled my nose. I just wanted to close my eyes and drift off to an island with her and that smell alone. The touch of her arms wrapped around my neck rubbing me gently made me want to take her right there in the hall.

"Com' on." She said grabbing my hand leading me up the stairs to her apartment.

She pushed the door to her apartment open and it was just as I imagined; a small cozy spot of heaven. There were brown plush sofas sitting next to large floor plants; a big flat screen TV that had to be no bigger than a 50" sat in the middle of the wall and she had bookshelves. There never would have been any bookshelves at my house seeing as though I didn't have any say so in how it was decorated and Mink never read anything besides a clothing tag. Her apartment was built much like mine with the bedrooms in the back and an island separating the kitchen from the living room but it was surely nicer than mine ever was.

"You want something to drink?" She asked walking towards the kitchen.

"Only you, Lasha." I replied pulling her arm towards me for a nice sloppy tongue-lashing.

Just as I reached my hand around to her protruding firm backside, my cell rang with a distinctive tone. I knew who it was and as much as I wanted to, I couldn't ignore the shit. It slowly pissed me off just thinking about answering but my fingers released her cheeks grabbing the phone anyway.

"Yeah?" My tone was almost angry.

"Boi, boi. What goes on?" Yolo's voice blared through the receiver.

"Not a thing. I was actually on my way out to you, man."

"Aiight. I'm at the office waiting on you bruh. We need to talk."

"Talk? That shit don't sound good." I replied stepping away from Lasha to focus on business.

"Don't worry 'bout it, just com' on through."

"I got you." I said hanging up the phone as my eyes shifted to Lasha spread out on the couch comfortably.

"You gotta go?" She asked revealing a smile more beautiful than gold.

"Yeah but I'll be back though. I wish I could spend the night with you, move in and never leave." My lips kissed her forehead softly.

"Naw, you got your son. You can't have him thinking you don't care about him too. My momma walked out on me and my daddy when I was eight years old and I never saw him again. I know what it feels like." Lasha replied batting her long dark eyelashes at me. "Besides I have school tonight. Can't get all the way to senior year and fuck up now."

"Yeah, you're right schoolgirl. What were you going for again?"

"I told you four weeks ago that I'm pre-med. So once I graduate then it's off to med school and then after that I'm quitting Home Depot's ass."

"Shit, maybe you can quit sooner than later."

"Huh? What are you talking about, Cesar?"

"Hmm. Nothing. Listen, I gotta ride, but I'm gonna call you later alright?" I kissed her soft succulent lips again, smacked her casually on her ass to feel that thang jiggle just a little and headed out the door.

The entire ride to the club, I could think of nothing but the night I saw Lasha there in that tight silver dress. She stood out, catching my eye faster than any of the females that surrounded her. It hit me that I blew her off all this time for Mink's lying and cheating ass when all the time I had a good woman sitting right in front of my face. Better late than never though and I'll be damned if I let her gorgeous ass slip through my fingertips. Lasha is definitely wifey material, something that I never even contemplated with Mink.

I pulled up into the empty lot of the club, parking right next to Yolo's black BMW. Grabbing the shoebox out from under the passenger seat as I did every day for the last for weeks, I exited the car and headed to the door using my backdoor key to get in. As usual, inside I found Yolo with his cell glued to his ear, chapping away to somebody about something. I didn't care to listen; whether it was business or pleasure I didn't give a fuck. I listen for my name, that's it. If it doesn't concern me, I ain't got no business in it.

"Ay, Yo. I just came by to drop off this change from the morning rush today." I said placing the shoebox down on the table and heading back towards the door. "We can rap later."

I hadn't been to the apartment Mink and I shared in weeks, since I've been working for Yolo. My son wasn't there, I figured there was no need for me to even lay eyes on Mink's triflin' ass. She was like a stray dog that if a stranger fed, would never go away, so I decided what better place to sleep and hang than the club, Passion. All I wanted to do was curl up in the backroom down the hall and catch a few z's before the 8am shift. My cell read 5:45am so I knew that was damn near not about to happen. Yolo sat at his desk in one of his tailor made suits like he had just stepped off the red carpet with Steve Harvey or somebody. It was early in the morning on a fucking Wednesday and this nigga looked like he was fresh off the movie screen. None of that flashiness interested me though. I was strictly here to get money and stack it high so I could get out of this shit unscathed. This business had a way of pulling you in too deep so I needed to make sure I stayed one foot ahead.

"Hold on my dude. Take a seat for a sec." He said holding the phone away from his ear pointing to the seats in front of his desk.

"Oh naw man, I just wanted to make the morning drop. Chill, we got plenty of time to talk." I replied hoping to skate out of the office and avoid his lengthy conversation.

His finger pointed up in the air and then down towards the seat in front of his desk insisting that I took a seat. My chest sank as I exhaled; walking back towards the chairs and plopping down, I realized that I was more exhausted than I thought. Sleep hadn't been my friend much these past few weeks but the money has been rolling in like clockwork. I hadn't paid the bills and rent since I hadn't been there but my son didn't need or want for anything and is enjoying a broke-free summer. Mink was probably heated since I knew Flava had to have told her by now that I got money. She probably thought she was about to be knee deep in my pockets by now. Haha. Crazy bird was always flying into shiny glass windows, thinking ahead of herself.

"Ah, my nigga." Yolo smiled as he slammed his cell down on the desk. "Playa, playa. I gotta say man; you have been doing your thing over there on the set, bringing in some serious revenue, dude. I'm impressed."

"It's nothing, dude. Just doing what I said I was going to do and trying to make it happen for my fam too, you know." I replied feeling my eyes become heavier and heavier.

"Yeah, yeah. But now that that's good over there, I don't think you need to monitor that on a daily anymore. I think it's time to get you on the trust factor making some real serious dough. You know what I mean?"

"Uh, naw Yolo. I don't follow."

"Ceasar, it's time to stop nickel and diming on my side hustle and step up with the big boys."

"Side hustle? Nigga, I thought this was what you did

all along." I laughed forcing myself fully awake to get the gist of his words.

"Naw, C. I just like to keep my hands in every aspect of getting money. Ya feel me? Never put all your eggs in one basket." He replied walking over to the long deep black bar in the far corner of the room. "Drink?"

"Naw, I'm good." I replied as he poured himself a stiff one. "So where's the real money at?"

"Why don't you catch a flight with me right now? You busy?" He said finishing what looked like a half a glass of Absolut.

"Catch a flight, right now? Man, what the hell is going on dude?" I tried to hold the bass in my voice, not allowing it to crack.

I wasn't afraid to fly or anything but it was known of Yolo that when you took flights with motherfuckas, your ass was liable to not come back. I didn't know if this nigga trusted me or not. I didn't know if he was trying to set me up or if I was paranoid. All I knew was that if push came to shove, I would fight my ass off to be the last man standing and good ol' Yolo would be taking that dirt nap instead of me. He was cool, but I could never put anything past anybody when dealing with money.

"Right now, nigga!" His echo rang loudly throughout the office. "The fuck is you scared of?"

"Never scared, Yolo." I replied calmly.

"Aiight then. You don't need to pack or take shit. How much is in the box this morning?"

"Almost four stacks."

"Good, take it. It's yours."

"What? You lettin' me have the pot, Yolo?"

"Dude, you've been bustin' your ass for these past few weeks. You took over a spot that was making no money and got it breaking two stacks a shift or better. How can I not reward some shit like that?" He said killing his cigar in the ashtray before walking to his office closet door. "Didn't you earn it?"

"Hell yeah! I was just makin' sure that you weren't bluffing or nothing; giving me the entire pot and all."

"My nigga." Every time he said that word, he sounded funny with him being Mexican and all. "You ready to take this flight, Cesar?"

"Not really but let's do it." I reluctantly agreed.

I stuffed the money down in my pocket and headed downstairs to wait for him outside by his car. I was nowhere near prepared for what he had in store for me nor did I have any idea where we were going. The only thing I did know was that I needed to keep my eyes and ears open just in case anything popped off. Yolo was cool but the truth was I didn't trust anybody outside of my son and myself.

Yolo met me at the black BMW, popping the locks on the doors from the button on his keychain. I slid back in the cream colored leather seats admiring the wood grain interior he must have had installed. *It must be nice.* I thought as I couldn't help but to wonder what the fuck would happen next. My mind felt like it was about to start playing tricks on me, having me paranoid and shit. When I was younger my mother used to tell me that I could always tell when I smelled bullshit, because my nose would turn up unknowingly whenever someone told a lie. I could never tell but I decided to put that theory to the test.

"So, where are we headed?" I asked nonchalantly.

"To Midway Airport then we're gonna hop a plane to Miami." He responded as he drove on.

"Miami? That's wassup. What's out there?"

"My other business."

"Shhhh, Yo, I feel you on being a man of few words and shit but straight up dog, where the fuck we going, dude?" I shifted my body to look the man in his face while keeping one eye on the road.

His laughter was sinister but I realized that I hadn't turned my nose up yet. I didn't smell bullshit anywhere in the air. I waited on him to finish getting a kick out of my question; the car went silent and he leaned back in his seat.

"What? You don't trust me?" He asked slowly.

"Hell, it ain't that. I just like to know what's going on. Ya feel me? I like to be abreast of the situation."

"Abreast huh?" Yolo chuckled again. "Sit back and relax, C. I wanna tell you a story."

**Thick thighs swayed and heels clacked as the ladies walked out of the white door and onto the empty and shiny wooden floor. There were six of them all lined in a row and all wearing the same thing, shiny gold masquerade masks paired with black-laced corsets and matching thin thongs. Their heels were a wedged sole and they had eight gold wings on the front of each shoe. As a young man I had never seen anything so sensual or sexy like that in my life but my pops decided that this was the night that I learned about the family business. I was like a kid in a candy store at only twelve years old, hoping I could control my manhood from standing at attention with all the ass that was in the air.

"Boy, pay attention. This shit may look like it's fun and games but make no mistake, this shit is real and this is how we get our money. You understand?" He asked placing his hand on top of my shoulder gripping firmly.

"Yes, sir."

"Now these females are for sale. They've completed their five year tenure with the company and now they are about to be auctioned off to the highest bidder. These are niggas that done been customers with the company for a long ass time so they all cool. But, you get to know them *first* before you invite them to an auction. Not everyone is allowed in. This some exclusive shit and this business is strictly word of mouth. You got that?" He schooled.

"Service? What service, Pop?"

"Yolo, when the time is right you won't have to ask me that question." He replied avoiding the question.

"Yes, sir. So what happens to them when the men get tired of them?" I asked.

"Hey after they're sold, the rest ain't our problem. Ya heard me?" My pops chuckled scratching the gray hair growing from underneath his chin. "But for the most part, cause the women are so young, the customers usually marry them…even though they still come back for some pay to play action."

"How young are they?"

"I don't go no younger than 17 if they are a runaway; 18 if they are looking for a daddy. You know what I'm talking about, son." He laughed.

"Yeah pop." I lied.

I had no idea what the fuck he was talking about. All I knew was that when the lights went out and the spotlight shined down on the middle of the floor where the ladies were standing, all the niggas in the room went buck wild. The ladies stood there as stiff as some of the Johnsons in the room, ordered by my pops not to move unless told. It was then that my pops became my hero. He was the one man in my life that not only never let me down but also always kept it real with me. Until this, I had not known what the family business was. I only knew that we had a ton of money and whenever I wanted something I got it every time.

My dad, who most called Sole, was a determined man, never letting anything or anyone stand in the way of the things he wanted. He was about 5'9" and always wore his hair low like mine. But he was more muscular than me, coming in at about 200 solid pounds. Mostly everything about him I favored except for that. He worked out about two hours a day every day; wanting to be one of those bodybuilding type of dudes. He was dark skinned with dark eyes and a temper that could only be seen if he got ticked off enough, which in my opinion wasn't often. It was crazy to me to have all that muscle and never really use it. I didn't need all that shit, though. My anger alone was enough to bust heads; I didn't need big dumb ass muscles to prove a point.

"Sole! Sole! Start this shit man!" A guy yelled from across the room.

"Man, sit yo horny ass down!" My dad demanded. "Alright, the bidding will start with the Asian persuasion, Lin Mei. We will start at $50,000."

Damn that was a lot of money for a nigga to purchase a woman. If my dad was getting these chicks for free that means that he was making nothing but profit in return. As the Asian chick was sold for $450,000, I started to think about all of the things I could do with that kind of money. My hands were itching much like my mom's when she feels she's in the presence of money. She was weird that way. It was then that I wondered what she would think if she knew that this was how Pops made his money; that was until I saw her walk in covering the prize girl with a red silk robe. It shocked me to know that she was in on the family business too, especially since she was a female.

My dad started this business before I was born but decided to expand upon it and move to the States when I was five. We lived in a three flat building in the middle of Chinatown just outside of the downtown area where no one would ever suspect that this kind of shit was going on in here, despite us being the only Mexicans around. During the day it was as quiet as a mouse and at night my Pops ran the most expensive brothel in the city. As I walked through the crowd of overactive men, I paid close attention to their demeanor and the way they were dressed. They looked like captains of the industry, presidents and CEOs of high-powered companies. They ranged in all different age brackets from hair club for men to the ones with milk still dripping from behind their ears. Most of them were drinking but for the most part they all smoked really long thick cigars. All of this went on in the basement of our building.

I looked over to see a small group of women in the crowd too; it was crazy to me. Women were there to buy women and do things with them too. I saw one in a skin tight business type of suit come up behind my Pops and run her fake fingernails along the back of his tailored made suit jacket. She looked like she was leaning in, trying to get a whiff of his cologne or something but whatever it was she had to go.

"Pops, you need me to do anything?" I asked running up to him at the podium.

"Naw, Yolo. Why don't you walk around and see if you can find your mother. She might need some help." Sole spoke shooing me away.

It annoyed the shit out of me that he let that woman continue to rub on him like that and my mom was somewhere nearby. Nonetheless, I walked off in the last direction I saw my mother headed with the third girl my Pops had sold. She was in the room with the white door preparing and packing the girl's belongings for her departure with her buyer. The girl was sitting in front of a dressing room mirror balling, crying her eyes out. She couldn't have been any older than eighteen years old.

"What's wrong mom? Is she okay?" I asked walking up to the girl staring her in the face.

My mom whisked her hand through her low-slicked back hair cut to relieve stress as she rushed to make sure the girls had all of their belongings before coming over to me.

"Leave her alone honey. Hey why don't you go play? I don't know why your damn daddy chose today to show you all this shit." Mom spoke with a bit of rage in her voice.

She was usually a very well kept together lady. My mom, Liv, was a short little thing coming in at about 5'3" and she couldn't have weighed more than a buck five, soaking wet. She was of Venezuelan decent with very beautiful angelic like features. Her parents disowned her when she married my black dad. When she talked to her friends about her parents, she always brought up the fact that they fucked up cause now she's richer beyond her wildest dreams and they could've been a part of that. There were never any regrets that I could tell though and she made sure every chick that approached my dad knew that. What she lacked in size definitely was made up for in her punch.

"It's okay Liv. He's not bothering me." The girl cried

wiping the tears from her eyes. "I'm just sad because I have to leave my baby behind. I can't take her because my handler doesn't want kids."

"Oh. Well you ain't got no momma that can take your baby?" I asked rubbing her arm to console her.

"Naw. I'm all she has. If she was a baby, he would've let me keep her but because she's ten years old he says if I bring her, she will have to fuck too." The girl cried even harder.

"Damn." It was all I could think to say.

"Momma. Momma what's wrong?" The woman's daughter, Bonnie, walked in from out of the bathroom asking.

"Nothing, Bonnie. Everything's gonna be just fine." She lied.

"Are we moving again?" Bonnie asked.

"No honey. Momma's just gotta go out of town this time. I'll be back for you though. I promise I'll be back." She lied again.

"This don't feel right momma. Yolo? Yolo, what's happening?" Bonnie turned towards me.

"Don't worry about it. Your mom's is gonna be good. You like it here with us right? We treat you good right?" I asked forcing her to focus her eyes on me and not her mother.

"Yeah, but—"

"But nothing. So let's go find you something to do. You can play dress up or something with my sister." I wiped the large tears flowing from her bronzed cheeks. "It'll be fun."

My mother looked up at me with a wink and a smile. She knew I would be a natural at this job, holding my own and stepping up to be the man of the situation. Out of all the years we've been rich, this is the only time that we've ever had a kid that came along for the ride. Bonnie had been with us since she was five years old and I've always found her to be a nuisance. But now I felt like I was her protector and confidant. She would need one when she realizes that her momma ain't comin' back at all.

We made our way up towards my sister, Dahlia's room, where everything was red and all kinds of girlish dolls and toys ruled the room. She and my mom had a thing for red. Inside, the room was empty. I looked around the room for her but she was nowhere to be found. Bonnie looked

around as well then gave up; plopping down on the guest
bed to continue her crying session. It wasn't like Dahlia to be
missing in action like that, especially at 2am in the morning.
There were noises on her balcony but I choked it up as
random night animals fooling around until the noises grew
louder.

"Dahlia what the fuck are you doing out here?" I
bellowed looking down at her sucking some bitch ass nigga
off in the beach chair.

"Yolo, what the fuck are you doing in my room?" She
retorted angry only due the fact that I was embarrassing her.

"You wanna be a fucking hoe, then be a hoe when
you grow up but right now you gon' keep them fucking legs
together." I snapped almost blacking out as I pulled her back
in the room by her hair. "You hear what the fuck I say?"

"I don't have to listen to you! You ain't my fucking
daddy!"

Something inside of me lost it. I started punching her
in her chest and stomach hard but not hard enough that I
forgot she was a girl. I just needed her to get the message
that I wasn't fucking playing with her ass. A few more
punches then I was done with her as she curled over crying

and clenching her midsection. I looked up, watching as that stupid ass nigga she was suckin' off climbed over the balcony trying to get the fuck out of dodge. I ran up to him before he was able to take his hands off the ledge and pounded his fingers until he abruptly let go.

"Ahh shit!" The dude bellowed as his ass hit the ground.

"Bring your ass back to this house and next time it'll be a bullet in yo ass nigga!" I barked as I shut the balcony doors locking them behind me.

"You have no right to tell me who I can and cannot fuck, Yolo. This is my fucking body." Dahlia pushed and punched me but her fists didn't phase me.

"I bet Pops has a right though. Maybe we should go tell him then."

"I don't give a fuck. Go tell daddy. Go on, go tell him." She said as I walked towards the door. "He's down the hall in the second bathroom with that ugly big booty bitch he's always smilin' at. I'm sure right about now he's really gonna give a fuck about what I'm stickin' in my mouth."

I turned to look her in her eyes for signs of a lie; usually I was a good judge of character about that kind of shit, especially when I'm heated. But I found no sense of deception. I looked over at Bonnie still crying her eyes out silently but watching the entire argument. My mind was going forty miles per hour and so were my feet as I raced down the hall to see if she was telling the truth. Before I could get to the bathroom I could hear the moaning and groaning coming from the room. At the door all that could be heard were the sounds of a woman, getting her back banged out. It was much like the sounds that my mother used to make back when they used to have sex; only muffled.

"Ay, Pops." I banged on the door. "Pops."

"Yolo?" He asked out of breath. "Boy get away from the door. Go to your room."

"Com' on Pops. Mom wants you. She says it's important." I shook my head listening to his body slap against hers. This nigga couldn't even stop fucking to speak to me.

"Boy get your ass on now!" He roared nearly shaking my soul.

As I walked away from the door headed back to Dahlia's room, my head was hung down low. I couldn't help but feel beyond disappointed in him and the way he was disrespecting my mom. It was then that I lost all respect for him. He was no longer the great man that I looked up to; he was no longer my dad. He was simply just that nigga Sole. **

"Damn that shit's deep man." I said as we boarded the plane.

"Yeah. My parents were murdered a few years later when I was sixteen. Been running the spot ever since, just expanded it cause I didn't want it in the same city where I sleep, you know. Now you know, where we're about to go." Yolo responded as he took his seat and straightened his suit jacket. "I got girls being sold every year now. They all get a maximum of 5 years and then they're out to the highest bidder before they get too old. I don't trip cause my livestock stays full. You feel me?"

"No shit, I feel you. So you took on your dad's business?"

"Aye...somebody had to keep the Delgado legacy alive."

"So what happened to your sister and the little girl?" I asked seeing as though I've never heard him talk about them.

"I sold them. They chose that life, spreading their legs and shit so they needed to get paid for it. Now they're living richer than me. Good riddance." He said as his facial expression grew cold.

His words were fucked up but they didn't surprise me one bit. Females were out here giving the shit away for free or little to nothing, so there was no difference. All I could think about as I sat back in my plush First Class seat and took the glass of white wine that the stewardess handed me, was how much money he said he got per sale. I could retire and never have to do this shit again. Then again, this shit just seemed too easy. A nigga could get used to this.

"Please turn off your phones..." The flight attendant began speaking as I pulled my phone out realizing I had almost fifty missed calls.

I gladly powered it off. Anything not to have to see Mink's thirsty ass in my call log.

Chapter 10- Mink

If this man thinks he can ignore me and get away with it, he was sadly mistaken. He knows good and damn well that I need money and for the past few weeks he's been trying to act like he doesn't know. Now it's the first of the month and the bills and rent are due all over again and he hasn't even contacted me to at least tell me if he will pay them or not. I didn't know if he figured that I knew about him hooking up under Yolo's business and was trying to hide the money from me or what but I had the one thing that would break his back. I had the one thing that he couldn't ignore even if he tried.

"CJ, have you called to speak to your daddy today?" I asked walking into my mother's house as she rolled her eyes at me.

"No. Dad said he would call when he made it back into town." My son responded with his face stuck in the new Need For Speed game my mom brought him for his PS3.

"Back into town? Where did your daddy go baby?"

"I dunno mom. He told me he was out of town when I talked to him yesterday. Why don't you ask him?" CJ said.

"Because...boy don't be questioning me. You ain't old enough to be questioning me. Just call your damn daddy boy."

"Mom, just call him." Cesar Jr. sounded so much older and wiser before his time.

We often went back and forth like this in playful banter before we actually got serious about our conversation. The only thing was, because he was a kid he didn't know that there was a time to play and there was a time not to. So he didn't realize that his words were actually pissing me off. My son was my best friend no matter how old he got. I loved him, in my eyes, he could do no wrong. I snatched that boy's cell and toggled through his contacts before pushing send on Cesar's cell number then tossed it on the bed. To catch him off guard, CJ needed to speak to his daddy first, warming the conversation up a bit before gracing him with my voice. I grabbed the wireless controller from his hands forcing him to focus on what I needed him to do while shooting him a serious look.

"Hey dad." CJ said snarling at me.

His attitude didn't phase me. I was getting what I wanted and that was all that mattered. I tossed the controller down on the bed at the same time CJ flopped back, listening on the phone and waiting for his chance to speak.

"Yeah dad, I know. I'm being good though. I'm listening and behaving grandma." He replied to whatever Cesar was drilling him about. "Dad. Dad. Hold on dad, mom wants to talk to you."

"Hey, Cesar." It wasn't the subtle approach I was hoping for as I irritably snatched the phone away from my annoyed son, who eagerly grabbed his controller and got right back in the game. "Where have you been?"

"Why would you include CJ in all this? He don't need to be in the middle of our shit." Cesar replied angrily.

"He's not in the middle. I just needed to talk to you but you wouldn't answer my calls. Why the fuck are you avoiding me?"

"Because your ass is toxic, Mink. I need some fucking air."

"Okay and while you're getting air, did you think about the fact that I have to still live in that apartment and soon so will your son? Did you think about the fact that the bills and the rent are now?" I snapped walking out of the room headed towards the bathroom so CJ couldn't hear me.

"Get a fucking job, Mink." His words barked through the phone as if they would bite my ear right off. "I've always got my son so you ain't even gotta bring his name into this but you...you need to get off your ass and your back."

"Cesar—"

"Mink, you don't do shit but take and take from people and never give. When are you gonna wake the fuck up?"

"But Cesar you don't understand. Give me a chance to talk. Let me explain—"

"You're done explaining, lying, and weaseling your way in and out of shit. I ain't got time for this, Mink. I'm out."

"Cesar! Cesar!" I screamed through the phone squeezing it tightly as if it would mush and ooze like putty through my finger.

Rejection was the one thing that I didn't take too well and Cesar knew that. So for him to just blatantly hang up on me without thought, only heightened the ball of rage I was already feeling inside from his absence. I tossed the phone on the sink like it was nothing as the crashing sound resembled the way my heart felt. My feelings usually got the best of me when I didn't get my way with someone. He was acting like he didn't love me anymore, like he had moved on but little did he know that I'm not going out like that. The only way that nigga is getting rid of me is if he kills me and that's real. I'll be damned if he takes my money, my dick, and my son.

"Ma? You done with my phone yet? I need to text somebody." CJ bellowed banging on the bathroom door like he was the SWAT team.

"Ugh, yeah boy." Disgust rang through my voice. "Here. If your daddy calls you let him speak to your grandma. Tell him she's got something to tell him."

"Okay." He dashed back into the room without a trace to get his text on.

Just because Cesar was being a douche bag about talking to me, didn't mean that my plan wouldn't be set in motion. One way or the other that man was going to come back to me and give me the lavish spending life that I deserve. I couldn't walk fast enough to the kitchen looking over catching my mom in the midst of preparing lunch for Cesar Jr. before she went off to work; homemade cheeseburgers and fries.

"Mmm, my fav. Can I have one ma?"

"Hell naw. Girl you better fix your own. These are for my grandbaby and I already gotta go before I'm late for work." My mom rushed to put the lid on the final Tupperware bowl before tossing them both on the top shelf in the fridge.

The creases of my lips curled over as they smacked together making the famous sucking sound that drove my mother insane. To keep us from doing it when we were younger she used to tell us it was the mating call of fast tailed little girls. If we didn't want to be labeled little whores we couldn't make that sound. It worked for Flava until she was grown but only lasted with me until I graduated eighth grade and sprouted booty and tits like it was wildfire that summer. Boys were on me like white on rice and the attention showed me just exactly what my power was.

"Listen ma, I need you to do me a favor." I began as I bit my lip hoping to sound as sincere as possible. This lady could sniff out a lie quicker than a crack head on the hunt for a fix.

"I ain't got no money, Mink. Now I done paid all my bills and the mortgage and since I moved from the suburbs a few years ago you already know the city ain't cheap. So you better gone and ask one of your little boy toys to hook you up cause I can't help you." She rambled.

"MA! It ain't about money, alright? Dang, why you always gotta take it there?" My voice was raised in anger.

She always took it there. My mother and I never really saw eye to eye so every chance she got she cracked on me. She was always saying little smart ass comments about my lifestyle and what not because she knew it pissed me off. I wanted to tell her that I was so sorry I wasn't her prize child, the one she always wanted. I was so sorry that I wasn't her precious Flava. Instead I kept my mouth closed. It was better to let her fester in her own words than to argue with her especially since I needed her to do something for me. As much as it pained me not to fire back at her, I brushed it off.

"I need for you to talk to Cesar and tell him that I'm pregnant...again." I recited in a somber tone tilting my head down towards the floor as I sat down at the old white country style kitchen table.

"Pregnant? Awe, Mink. Now why did you go and get yourself in a predicament like that when you can barely take care of the one you got?" She slowly slid into the seat across the table from me shaking her head in dismay. "You ain't lying are you?"

"Lyin—, no! Ma! Why would I lie about something like that?" I slowed my anxious breathing. "I'm about to bring another one of your grandbabies into the world and that's all you can say to me?"

"Ugh...okay, Mink. Well I hope he takes care of this one too; because if you ask me CJ don't even look like him. This one might not look like him either. Flava said you were messing up with a good man but I sure didn't believe her."

"What the hell is that supposed to mean ma?"

"It means you wouldn't know a good thing if it slapped you in the face, knocked you unconscious then woke you up again staring you square in the eye." She laughed as she rose from the table to wipe down her marble counter.

"Wait, I thought you didn't like Cesar." I asked pressing my lips together smacking them again.

"I never said I didn't like him. I just didn't like the lifestyle you all lead. But he seems to have his head on straight enough to take care of his son. I don't know what it is you are doing."

"Okay you know what ma, I gotta go. Do you think you can just manage to tell Cesar that when you catch him on the phone with CJ later. Can ya do that, huh?" I asked walking towards the dining room trying to make a dash for the front door.

"Yeah, Mink. I'll do that for you. Just make sure you know what you're doing. Now can you do that?" A sniffle came from her face.

I couldn't see her face clearly because her head was down and she was keeping busy; focusing her eyes to the counter like it was about to disappear on her. Even though I heard sudden faint sniffles, I couldn't make out if she was crying or just blowing away allergy issues. Either way, her emotion was like the freezer at a grocery store to me, cold as hell.

"I know what I'm doing ma. I'm saving my family." I said walking towards the front door. "Call me after you've talked to him please."

"You ain't gonna say goodbye to your son?"

"He'll be alright. He's being a game head right now

anyway."

I scurried out of the door before she was able to make a smart remark that would undoubtedly piss me off. Eager to see what the day had in store for me, I jumped into Cash's car; loving the fact that he was willing to drive me around at the drop of a hat when I needed him to. He didn't trust me well enough with his car yet but I was working on that too. Soon, I was gonna have this nigga living off the juices of my pussy so much that I got the keys to his house he claimed he had in the Hamptons of New York with no problem.

"You all done now?" Cash asked revving up the sun bright yellow Mustang and taking off.

"Well, I thought maybe we could go shopping. You know you like this ass looking good." I laughed hysterically.

"I bet you did think that." He smirked as we began turning down 95th in the direction of Chicago Ridge mall. "I got something to do today though, Mink. I can't play your man today."

"What the fuck you mean you can't play my man? Nigga you belong to me whether you like it or not."

"Naw, that dude you staying with belongs to you.

Remember?" He snarled.

"Ugh, why do you keep bringing that fool up? He ain't got nothing on you and you already know that."

"Don't feed me bullshit, Mink. I know what I am to you and I'm cool with that. Just know that when I'm tired, a nigga is gonna move on." He snapped. "Trust and believe."

"And just what do you think you are to me, Cash?"

"Your fuck boy. It's cool, though. Not every nigga can lay this steel like I do, ya feel me?"

We both chuckled. My chuckle was mainly because he thought he laid the pipe better than any nigga I've ever been with. I didn't really give a shit what his chuckle was about. To keep from laughing sidesplittingly, I turned my attention out the window.

"So is you trickin' or what, nigga? I ain't got all day and time definitely is money." I retorted quickly bringing the conversation back to the question at hand. "A bitch needs a new bag."

"Hmm. Why don't you come and put your head on my lap for a little while." Cash smiled reaching his hand around letting it rest gently on the back of my headrest while the other maintained the steering wheel.

My head swayed his way gradually leaning into his chest allowing it to roll down to his lap. His jeans were like sandpaper against my soft skin and even though I was in no mood for this I wasn't going to pretend that I didn't know why I was down there. My fingers made their way to his zipper, pushing his pants down just enough to reach in and pull out his massive meat. It was cute that he thought that he was bigger than Cesar even though he wasn't. I didn't give a fuck what he thought because what he thought didn't matter. As I adjusted my body, bringing my knees on the seat sitting in a childlike pose and lowered my mouth around his meat, all I could think about was how much money he was about to drop once his nut filled inside my jaws.

I giggled the whole way through at the thought of all the fresh new shit I was about to make this nigga get me. It didn't matter if it was his rent money or not, as long as he was spending that cash that's all I cared about. Now if he could just get his mind off of trying to wife me, I could have it all and still get whatever Cesar had to place at my feet.

Chapter 11- Cesar

The orange Southwest Airlines plane landed back at Midway and as the wheels stumbled to hit the pavement, a piece of me stumbled with it. I loved my city but Miami was for damn sure a well-deserved vacation; even if it was only for no less than 24 hours. I walked past the cockpit stepping off the plane, tired as hell and ready to lay it down for a few hours before I went to check the spot over in Marquette Park. Yolo was a few people behind me yapping away on his phone again as I walked towards the terminal and caught a seat.

"Aye bro. Let's go." Yolo pointed as he walked off.

With no luggage, we hailed a cab quick as hell as soon as we made it to the arrivals waiting area. After all of that money he had just gotten, I was wondering just how well he was intending to pay me. All I could think about was Yolo had to have made over $2 million dollars easily from all that ass he had housed up in that high rise out there. After hearing that story about his dad, I couldn't even fathom what he had going on down there until I walked in to that huge condo with about ten different women walking around half naked and fine as hell. He had all nationalities too, never discriminating, and sold five of them to the highest bidder at a round table discussion setting as the chicks walked around the room advertising themselves.

"Man that was a wild ass ride, Yo. I gotta admit it was the shit, making me not wanna get back on the plane." I said as he hung up the phone stuffing it down into his pocket.

"Yeah, you liked that shit, huh? How would you like to do it every month?" He asked keeping a straight face, never looking over to me.

"Huh? Every month?"

"I'll even let you pick the new recruits."

"What? Man, Yolo you fucking my head up with all this shit here dude."

"I'm dead ass serious. I've got so much going on that I've been looking for help with all this shit. Trying to expand to New York and everything. But you can't let everybody in your business; you know what I mean and them disloyal ass motherfuckas around me gotta be weeded out ya feel me?" Yolo gritted his teeth in anger. "I can't even trust my own fam."

"Yeah that shit's crazy."

"But you. You came to me from my baby and if she vouched for you then you a nigga I fucks with. Ya feel me, boi?"

"Yeah, I got you Yo. I'm touched and all, you know. I just really wasn't trying to get deep in this shit like that. I really just wanted to get my feet wet and stay above ground until I could find a gig." I tried to keep my voice as humble as possible so he knew that I wasn't ungrateful for the opportunity he had blessed me with.

"Just get your feet wet huh?" He sneered as we made it back to his car, popping the alarm. "Get in. I'mma drive you home."

"Home? Naw, Yo. I'mma go back to the club and get my car and some rest." I lied.

Actually, I couldn't wait to get a moment alone so I could call Lasha and hopefully get her to stay home from work to spend the day with me. I was working off little to no sleep but I didn't give a fuck. I needed that woman in my arms. If she was cocaine then you could say that I was hooked. Something about her had me locked in a trance and

I didn't care. She gave me everything I had been missing all these years.

"Aight. I'mma drive you to the club but you ain't stayin' there nigga. Go home and face that bitch. Get her out of your life for good. A bitch like that ain't good for shit but getting on her knees whether she's your baby momma or not." Yolo snapped.

"Yeah...I know." It was all I could say. Shit he was right.

"Listen bro. I got a package that I'm personally gonna deliver to you later on though. So stay near the phone cause when I call you, I'll be on my way to you."

"Aight, no doubt."

As we neared the club, my mind shifted over to the reality of his words. That bitch had to go. But I didn't know just how that was going to happen without hurting my son. She was toxic for him too but he might not be old enough to realize that. Leaning back in the seat as Yolo whipped into the parking lot of the club, her face flashed before my eyes. Lasha.

"Aight, playboy. I'm gon' holla at you in a few hours." Yolo said as I exited his car.

"Aight."

Eager as hell, I reached into my pocket for my phone and quickly dialed her number while unlocking the truck door. The phone just kept ringing and ringing. No answer. I tried it again but got the same thing. A part of me began to get frustrated. It wasn't like her not to answer the phone regardless of what she was doing. Calming my breathing and anxiety, I just figured maybe she went to the bathroom or was in the shower or something. Even though every fiber of my being just wanted to go clean off believing that she might have been laughing in the face of another dude, I revamped my thoughts. She wasn't Mink, she was a good girl and I knew she wouldn't do that to me. Still, my mind was playing tricks on me.

I rang her number again and again but still nothing. My legs couldn't enter the car fast enough and hit the streets like a racecar demon. Swerving in and out of lanes and dodging red lights I got to her apartment in no time. I headed up to the front door checking out the buzzer before I touched it. My hand was itching to push the hell out of that damn thing until my fingers bled, but I took a second to breathe and then I pushed it slowly.

"Who is it?"

"It's me girl. Buzz me up." A sigh of relief exited my body.

"Hey baby. Com' on up."

She buzzed me in and as I opened the door, racing up the stairs skipping one step each way to the second floor, I knew I had to have been tripping. But having been cheated on as long as I have, I was already awaiting the bullshit and anticipating finding out bad news. At her door, I knocked lightly trying to gain my composure so I didn't lead the conversation with my insecurities.

"Hey baby." She kissed me smelling like some kind of strawberry watermelon scent.

It did nothing but make me hungry for her ass. I took her right there, closing the door behind me. I took her, grabbing her hand pulling her back into my embrace before she could walk off and make up any kind of excuse that she had to do something. I took her, right there in the small corridor that separated her living room from her doorway. We didn't need a bed, the floor was our bed. All I needed was her and she needed only me to survive. I was tired of not having her to myself.

The veins popped out of my hands because I was

grasping her so hard, clenching every bit of juicy thickness in my hands. I squeezed it so tightly that she excreted a small moan hoping for solace but she knew to take it like a big girl. There were bigger better things that she needed to hold that moaning for. Meanwhile I massaged her backside like there was no tomorrow. My lips engulfed hers and if my body could wrap around hers and become one it would have. She didn't know the kind of built up tension I was going to release into her but soon she would certainly find out.

"Mmm, baby. Wait. Wait please." Lasha begged placing her arms on my shoulders pushing extra lightly as if she really didn't want me to stop.

"Whassup baby." I responded, whispering deeply through kisses moving down to nibble roughly on her neck.

"I need to tell you something. Actually a couple of things but one is more important than the other." She said hoping to calm down my lustful advances.

"I can't help it baby. I want you so bad. Can't it wait?"

"No...no it can't baby. Please, we need to talk." She winced sounding disappointed in herself that she stopped me.

Lasha grabbed me by the hand, leading me to her microfiber couch and plopped down next to me. I tried my best not to grab any part of her in a sexual manner while she was trying to be serious and talk. That didn't keep me from licking my lips wanting to munch the fuck out of that pussy or bury my face in between those perfectly perky C cups.

"What I say may come as a shock to you but I need you to know that I didn't try to lead you on in any way and that I hope this doesn't change anything between us." Lasha began.

"Okay girl. You're scaring the shit out of me. What is it?" I sobered up from my drunken lustful trance quick.

"I'm...I'm...."

"Girl if you about to say what I think you about to say you better back the fuck up off me right now cause I swear to God, I'm gonna beat the brakes off your ass..."

"Will you shut the fuck up so I can speak? Damn!" Her irritation resonated across her face.

"Aight...shoot." I leaned back into the soft couch hoping I didn't have to whoop ass and blow chunks at the same damn time.

Right then my phone rang. It was Yolo and I already knew what that meant. I had just left this nigga no less than a few minutes ago and already he was calling to handle some more business. My mind was telling me no, not to answer the damn thing but on the other shoulder I was thinking that business always came before pleasure, even if I was horny as hell and trying to get some.

"Ugh...hold that thought." I told her as I placed the phone to my ear. "Yo, what up?"

"Yeah, C, change of plans. Something's come up and we need to take care of the lil spot over there on 65th. I'll hand you your luggage there. Meet me at the spot over there by opening tonight, ya feel me?" He growled sounding raspy as hell.

"You good dude?"

"Yeah. Just meet me there tonight. Ya heard?"

"Yeah, yeah. No doubt, Yo." I assured him.

I didn't know what was bugging him but I wasn't going to let it concern me right then. My mind was inquiring about the information that Lasha had for me. Stuffing the phone back down in my pocket, I leaned back once again and this time taking a long deep breath, exhaling it slowly.

"So what you needed to tell me so bad that couldn't wait, Lasha." I asked wondering if I really wanted to know the answer.

"Well I was going to make you guess but since I'm not a chick that likes to play games and you seem upset about something, I'm just gonna come out with it." She replied nervously. "I'm a...a...ugh! Why is this so hard?"

"Yeah you fucking tell me why it's so hard. Just say it, man." I sighed heavily looking up at the ceiling. "Are you a fucking man?"

"What? Nigga hell no! I was going to say that I'm a virgin!" Lasha snapped as she stood up crossing her arms and tossing me a fucked up look. "I'm mad you thought I was going to say that. Do I look like a fucking man to you?"

"Hell naw, baby! I just didn't know what you were going to say and you were taking all day, shit that's the first thing that came to mind." My facial expression read of relief. "But now that that's over... a virgin? Wow. How did you pull that off?"

"Um, well let's see. I did it by keeping my legs closed and minding my pussy." She laughed. "Naw but truthfully my daddy really didn't allow me to go out much. I was too busy training and studying so as I grew into an adult it just stuck with me not to date or at the very least, give my cookies away."

"Training? What kind of training you talking about?" I asked curiously. "Wait...so you don't get horny or even think about it now that you're old enough to make up your own mind?"

"Can't miss what you never had, Cesar." Lasha giggled before looking away then turned back to me allowing her beautiful pearly whites to shine through.

"Damn woman! You had me thinking it was something serious. Virginity, I can handle that. So...do you have any idea of when you'd be ready?" I pressed.

"No, just whenever I feel like I'm ready." Lasha smirked and winked one of her eyes.

"Oh...ok." There was no denying my disappointment. "But I don't give a fuck; I'll wait as long as you want me to. Maybe I can make this a little more special for you."

"How special?"

"Special enough that I want us to be together, move in together, raise my son together, and maybe have some more babies." I reached my hand up to her head pulling her in for a few sweet kisses.

"Babies? Eh...that sounds nice. But for now we can just try moving in together." Lasha licked her lips returning the sweet kisses to my lips.

"Why you say it like that? You do want kids right? Don't you like them?"

"Yes baby, of course I do. I'm just not sure if I'm ready to have any of my own yet. That's all." She sat back in the couch away from me. "I've just got a lot going on right now."

"I understand. You wanna be comfortable in your career as a plastic surgeon or pediatrician or whatever it is you wanna be."

We laughed hard. Her smile was more breathtaking every time I saw it. I could tell by her body language that I had kind of freaked her out about the whole thing but I knew in my heart that she was the one for me and I wasn't willing to lose that. We could move in together but eventually she would be my wife and she would have my kids. Period. And I knew just how to get her.

"Well, um, I do know something we can do since you

are saving yourself."

"Oh yeah. What's that?"

"Hmm." I smirked looking over at her sitting there. "Do you have to work today?"

"No."

"Good, cause I what I'm about to do right now is gonna take some time and I'm going to need for you to trust me." I winked. "Do you trust me?"

"Should I have any reason not to?"

There was always something so mysterious about her but I guess that's what attracted me the most. She was dressed in an all black jumpsuit that was fitting her body nice and closely. Her curves presented themselves to me as if they were calling my name. I had to try even though I felt she might object to my advances. Gradually I reached down removing her fluffy white house shoes from her lovely size eight painted toes, dropping them to the floor. My lips touched them sending gentle pecks from one perfectly red painted toe to the next. Lasha giggled low as if she didn't want me to hear it, as I forced her legs onto the couch positioning my body in between her legs.

My hand reached up to her long curled hair, running my fingers through it massaging as I came down to her cheeks and then her neck. They ran across her skin slowly giving a slight tickle, just enough to send her pussy the message it had been waiting to receive forever. She leaned her head back closing her eyes and exhaling silently letting me know she was ready for me to give her what her body yearned for. With one hand, I maneuvered her pants and unbuttoned them. With the other hand, I crawled under her shirt to caress the breasts that she had arched up in the air for me.

"What do you want, Lasha?" I whispered watching as her body began to gyrate and lose control.

"I...I don't know, baby." She responded.

"Mmm, that wasn't the right answer."

One hand flicked her nipples gently yet rapidly, her breathing heightened. I finally released her pants from its worn position and wiggled them down her voluptuous backside first before pulling them down those thick thighs and off, tossing them behind me. Moving much like a snake would, I maneuvered my body on top of hers allowing her to search my body with her fingertips rolling over the bumps and curves of my muscles.

"Cesar..." Lasha whispered as my kisses made their way down to the top of her slit pulling her purple panties down as I did. "Cesar...I...maybe we should—"

I gave her skin one good lick before she could finish as she quivered by the sensation. She was clean shaved, which made me think that she was waiting for me; waiting for the day that I placed my tongue on her clitoris. I wanted to show her everything she would be getting when she became my wife. I wanted to prove to her that I could be the man she needed me to be inside of the bed as well as out. Her panties out of the way, I used my tongue and lips to stimulate the extremely sensitive areas of her vulva and clitoris. My tongue circled, changing it up a bit, while I listened to what made her moan.

"Turn over." Since this was her first time, I wanted to make sure I maximized her experience that way if she ever had anybody else taste her juices, nobody else would compare to me.

Lasha was up on all fours poking that fat ass booty out like she was ready to twerk it out on my face. If she did I wouldn't have been mad. I got on my knees, came up behind her and put my arm around her gripping that ass firmly rubbing my front against her back. I leaned down breathing heavily on her plumped cheeks then went to nibble on them as well. Her moaning became erratic as I listened for faint direct instructions to stop or that I was being bad. My tongue made its way out of my mouth and right on the opening of her ass opening, making sure not to penetrate though, only giving her enough to tease.

"Oh my fucking...AH!" She screeched before burying her face in the couch cushion.

She threw her ass back giving the hint that she loved what I was doing to her and that she might have wanted me to keep going, but I'm not going to. I pulled back immediately letting the air breeze on her skin remaining perfectly still and quiet. Stopping a foreplay action will keep in her mind that I desire her and she'll be thinking about this all day. The task is small, didn't really do much of anything, but it's effective nonetheless. I didn't want to treat her like any other woman, because she was anything but.

"Lay on your back and spread your legs as wide as you can get them." I demanded sensually.

Once she had done as I had told her, I started from the top kissing her tender lips passionately, massaging her tongue with mine; moving from her lips, breathing and kissing lightly on her neck, then moving in to nibble on her earlobe. I was grateful that she allowed my hands to wander and caress her. I began kissing her down her body, in random places; kissing and sucking on her salacious big brown nipples, down her front, then to her belly button, spending a few seconds there. Her reaction let me know, it is one of her most sensitive areas. Flicking my tongue around it a few times, she giggled; placing a smile on my face as well before I made my way all the way back down to kiss her vulva, only to kiss around it to tease. I licked her thighs in a circular motion and licked the undercut of her backside then made my way back to her juicy pussy; blowing on it very lightly.

I took my tongue and caressed her vulva with it, from her womanly opening to her clitoris stroking a sensitive bundle of nerves that will do wonders. I took my tongue, laid it flat, and rubbed it up and down the entire length of her vulva. All of this is for the sole purpose of teasing her to make her want it more, which will make the experience for her all the more pleasurable. She hesitated for a second but then she took her hands and placed it on the back of my head and pressed it deep into her wetness. It was dripping. I bet she didn't think she could do that. I bet she didn't think I could make her splash all over herself but I know one thing, she was loving every minute of it.

At that moment, I plunged my tongue into her pussy, allowing it to wander, pressing against her walls letting it find what it can, but not for too long. Just as her hips were beginning to gyrate into my mouth I shot up to the clitoris fast. Knowing it was impossible, I damn sure tried to get my tongue inside of there, going slow at first then picking up the pace. It was mostly a rapid licking-up motion. I was imagining a candy bar melted in the wrapper and after the bar was all gone I still wanted the chocolate on the paper but the only way to get it off was to lick it off. Lick it off like my life depended on it.

Her pussy was pretty. It wasn't one that had tons of miles on it after being beat up for so many years. No, this one made me salivate like a hungry dog. I considered licking a pussy as pretty as this an art, something that I was proud of. Her breath quickened and her voice began to elevate. She pressed harder on the back of my head digging her nails in slightly but not enough to cause pain. My tongue was frantic and wild moving in the most rapid quick successions that I could conjure. No matter how long it took, no matter if the bottom of my tongue went numb and started to hurt, I would not stop until she had reached her climax and even then I would suck on it gently.

"O-O-O-OOOOO!" She bellowed louder than any

bomb I had ever heard explode. "Baby, shit!"

I would suck long enough to allow her to catch her breath and then I would start right up again but only for a second to keep her pulsating for me. She loved it, I could tell. I desperately wanted to slide two fingers inside of her but I would be damned if my fingers got that action before my beef did. I slowed my tongue flicking and backed away slowly but not before leaving a few extra kisses behind. I rubbed my lips in her juices for a few seconds making sure to leave every bit of her scent on me. Her taste drove me insane, like she had been eating sweet licorice all day and now it was excreting out in flavors from her. The results I was looking for were monumental, just what I was expecting. She climaxed harder than any other chick I had ever been with and as I watched her breathe like she had just finished running for her life, I felt damn proud.

"Ooo, Cesar! I can't believe I just let you do that. So many other guys have been begging to do that to me just to get me to fuck and I just let you do it with no hesitation." Lasha huffed rubbing her tits for added pleasure. "If I had known that's how good it felt I would've done it a long time ago."

"Yeah, but I'm glad you didn't. Now you can say that

I was your first." I smiled.

"My first, my last, and my only." She smirked turning on all fours crawling over to me like a lioness hunting her prey. The look was stamped in her eyes. "Let's do it baby. I want you to be the one."

She whispered amiably in my ear before nibbling on it. Her tongue felt as soft as her body did, like silk. I wanted to take her right there, give her body exactly what it was asking for. She wanted me to, rubbing on my chest then making her way down to my jeans to catch a sneak peak at my package. The bulge shocked her as she jumped back a little. I planted my feet firmly on the ground, staring at her in her eyes to signal that that was all me baby.

"Lasha, you think you're ready for this right here?"

"I'm a big girl. I can take it baby." She smiled looking at me with those big sultry eyes.

My chest went up then down as I took a deep breath wondering if I was making the right decision. "As much as I would like to be the one to break that pretty thang wide open right now, I'm gonna have to pass."

"Huh? Pass? Are you serious?" Her look suddenly went from angelic to evil in under a second. "You just eat pussy then. Is that it?"

"Naw girl." I laughed hysterically. "I wanna respect your wishes and your body. I want you to give it to me on our wedding night."

"WHAT? Okay, Cesar now you're trippin'." Lasha laughed rising up from the couch.

"Listen I gotta go but I'll be back later though. I gotta get my shit from this other place and take care of some business and then I'll be home tonight baby." I kissed her lips gently. "Alright?"

"Wait, you're moving in...tonight?"

"Is that a problem?"

"Oh...uh, no. I just wanted to be sure that's what *you* wanted to do, baby." She said looking confused.

"Aye, are you gonna be my girl? Are we gonna do this thing or what? Cause I don't got time to play games. Period." My voice was stern and forward.

"Yes, yes baby. Without a doubt!" It was the best reply she could've given me.

"Okay then that's what I'm talking about. So you

need to get used to the fact that you are gonna be my wife. I want you, you got me open and that's all that matters." My lips pecked hers once more. "Alright?"

"Yes, baby. I got you."

"Good." I grinned before slapping her on the ass and heading to the door. "I'll call you later baby."

Chapter 12- Time to render

**Cesar

After spending the day with the movers, I made it over to the spot just in the nick of time. It was 7:55pm and the spot didn't open until 8pm so no product was sold yet. When I pulled up, Yolo was already there, sitting in his car with the window cracked midway as smoke seeped out the top. I parked and walked up to it getting in the passenger side. He sat silently for a few minutes not even moving aside from the cigar smoke being blown from his lips. The car was silent as well. The only thing that could be heard was the sound of summer bugs dwindling down for the night outside.

"I think I need to shut this joint down, C. What you think?" Yolo said between puffs.

"Man, I think you need to chill for a minute at least. You know you just got it back up and running and it's only been a couple of weeks if you thinking about the income." I contested.

"Naw, nigga. It ain't about the dough. It's about

them motherfucking cops down there parked on the corner. Mo called me the other day and told me that they've been watching for a minute."

"What you think it's about? They aren't Narcs or else they would've been came and shut down the joint. Plus they don't use patrol cars. That's a fucking patrol car, Yo." I said slapping my thigh feeling like someone had to have been talking too much starting with one of them fools inside. Well it's almost 8pm, Yo. That's probably just what they're waiting on too; for the shop to open.

The line began forming in front of the door quicker than I realized and Yolo peeped it too. Even if we wanted to shut the place down for a few days we couldn't start tonight because the fiends were forming a line around the corner. Yolo kept his eyes down the street though making sure that he didn't sleep on the people watching him.

"Naw. My other business is more important than this one. I think it's time to shut it down. Besides I got sets in higher paying spots that I don't have to rebuild and those two fuck-ups in there fucked this shit up to begin with." Yolo spat putting his cigar out in the ashtray. "Especially after what you told me when you first got up in there. Shits nasty man and they're worthless skimming money off the top like

I'm stupid. Ya feel me?"

"I hear you, Yo. Let me go see what these jerks are doing." I exited the car.

"Hold on bro. I'm right with you." Yolo responded.

We walked up to the house passed the fiends and into the door. The operation was well organized. Them heads knew if they fucked up in line they wouldn't be getting shit today so they knew to be patient and on their best behavior. Inside the house, Mo was sitting on the couch doing what he did best, relaxing his ass. Meanwhile, Drake was already at the door setting up shop and getting ready to open. Yolo stood in silence observing the way the business was conducted turning his eyebrow and his nose up every chance he got. Drake was just about to open the door when there was a strong pounding on the other side.

We all looked over at each other. We knew that there was no way a fiend would be knocking on the door like that. It could only be one kind of person. Yolo put his hand up signaling for none of us to move. He walked towards the door opening it with a fake bright smile on his face. Two of the Chicago PD's finest stood at the door, one white and one black and they were both peeking their heads in the screen door trying to get a good look of what and who was inside.

"You boys sure got a lot of activity going on in here." The white cop said grabbing his belt to straighten it.

"Yeah, well we're popular dudes, officer." Yolo responded stepping out onto the porch as the two chuckled briefly.

"I'm just saying one might be inclined to say that there might be too much action going on here. Wouldn't you think?" The officer retorted.

"Have you ever wanted to just drop everything you're doing and take your lovely wife on a cruise to the Bahamas?" Yolo spat looking past the cops and into the street. "How would the wife like to do that, say, once a month?"

"Uh...she'd probably like that very much. But it ain't gonna happen." He answered.

"Maybe if you checked the garbage can more often, it could. And that goes for you too bro." Yolo pointed to the black cop.

"The garbage can?"

"Yeah, the one down the street on the corner next to the mailbox. It should be filled by noon on the first of the month, every month we're in operation that is." Yolo smirked. "And I'll tell you what, since it's already the middle of the month, I'm going to pay you for this full month."

"Well, sounds like we're about to go down the street and we'll sit there until the garbage man comes." The officer said before signaling for his partner to follow him away from the house.

"Aye, Yo. You really gonna pay these motherfuckas off man?" I asked walking up to the door letting the fiends walk up one by one to get their orders.

"Sometimes you gotta pay to play my dude. But it's not gonna matter after tonight."

"Why's that?" I asked but got no answer.

We all sat there in squander for the next 2 hours and after the last fiend had counted his change and gotten his fix, we shut it down locking the doors. Drake was at the door counting the scratch, Mo looked as if he was zooted off of that dope himself. Yolo noticed it too and figured those two had to have been skimming product off the top as well, which in turn took more money out of his pocket and that's another reason why his pockets were always short as ever before Cesar got there.

"Count that motherfucking money nigga." Yolo snapped becoming disgusted by the smell festering in the smoldering hot summer.

"I'm done Yolo. I'm done. You can come and get this money."

"How much is it?"

"Man about $8000 is here." Drake growled.

"Alright. Put that in a black garbage bag and here take this eight grand here and put it in there too then take it to the trash on the corner. Move!" Yolo bellowed scaring the shit out of him, counting out eight thousand dollars in cash from his pocket.

Drake got gone quickly realizing how pissed Yolo was this evening.

"Aye, Yo. Profit's gone up man. It can't do nothing but get better from here." I assured him looking at the box of emptied product, feeling a bit proud.

"Yeah, that's why you're my new right hand man." He chuckled before reaching behind his back. "Aye Mo!" He yelled.

Boom. Boom.

Before Mo could gather himself to look up he had planted two slugs in his chest. His half naked body slumped over to the side as his blood oozed on to the couch. His fingers were still balled up from the previous position. Mo's pants darkened in the front seat area. That nigga never saw it coming.

"Oh! Damn, Yo. What's good?" I asked slowly turning to him.

"Shop closed bro. We got bigger and better fish to fry and these niggas were nothing but another hand in my pocket. Fucking liabilities." Yolo said leaning against the wall behind the front door. "Especially that nigga Drake, thinking just because I took his runaway ass in from off the streets that he could fuck me over. Naw, it ain't going down like that homey."

He was waiting for Drake to come walking his ass in the house. I couldn't do shit but stand there and wait for this nigga's brains to be splattered all over the living room, without him even seeing it coming. That shit was one hell of a way to go out but there wasn't shit I could do about it. Yeah, I thought they were some lazy ass worthless pieces of space but I wasn't sure they deserved to die for it. But in the streets its kill or be killed and if Yolo felt like they needed to be rocked to sleep then that's what it was.

"Where the fuck is this nigga at man?" Yolo asked bringing his arm back down to his side.

"Shit, I don't know."

"Go check it out, C."

Reluctantly, I walked out the door keeping my eyes and ears open just in case. I walked off the stoop and out to the sidewalk leering down the street to see if I could see the nigga by the garbage can but all I saw were the cops getting there trash. I turned looking the other way and there he was speed walking down the street looking suspect as hell; looking like he had a whole heap of shit in his drawers.

"Aye, Drake!" I yelled. "Where the fuck you going, dude?"

"Uh...I gotta go! I'll be back!" He yelled back before taking off running.

"Aye, motherfucka! Come back!"

There were kids outside still playing and enjoying their freedom. If it weren't for that I would emptied my clip trying to put on in his ass. I walked back into the house to deliver the bad news to Yolo. He was heated but he soon shook it off.

"Yeah, that nigga can run but he can't hide. He probably was walking back and heard the gunshot and knew what was up." Yolo said sucking his teeth. "It's cool though. I'mma get that motherfucka."

Yolo took out his phone and made a call to the Cleaning Crew to come and scrap up Mo's body from off the couch. He even indicated that he wanted the nigga to get a proper burial; whatever the fuck that meant. After the call, he told me to help him search the house for anything else that was of importance. When there was nothing, we left locking the door securely behind us. The Cleaning Crew knew how to handle things after that. They were the ones who made problems disappear and were a group of chicks that Yolo had been friends with since high school. He entrusted them with his legal endeavors but most of all his life. Even though I had gotten used to working the trap after a few weeks, I was kind of glad to see it go. I hated working in one spot on the streets on an everyday basis. That's how motherfuckas got caught up.

"C. This shit right here is for you bro." Yolo grinned handing me a big black suitcase that he'd gotten from the back seat.

. "Oh yeah? All for me huh?"

"You earned it and they'll be plenty more where that came from if you run the spot down in Miami for me. You'll only fly out once or twice a month."

"Yo, man. I can't even thank you enough for this shit right here man. This shit is truly a blessing. I got me a new girl and I wanna show her that I can provide and handle my business." I said shaking up with him.

"Oh yeah? Is she a good girl?"

"Most def bro. One of the best." I countered.

"That's wassup, dude. Take that joint right there and get her a house, maybe a baseball ring or something, eh?" He said as he headed to the driver's side of his car. "Call me tomorrow. We'll do something."

"I got you and thanks!" I roared watching as he sped off faster than a roadrunner.

I looked down at the suitcase just imagining how much money was inside but I didn't have to wonder for long because there was a note taped to the handle:

C,

Enjoy this, you earned it. Here's $250k and there is much more where that came from if you stick with me.

Yo!

As I loaded my belongings into the truck, a large black van pulled up alongside of me. I was told never to speak to them, never even look up into their faces. Never questioning it, I just did as I was told and I literally never saw them. The side door of the van slid open as quickly as it shut. Two of the cleaners jumped out, walking past me fast as hell while the driver drove off. Just as I was about to duck into the truck to mind my business and get going, I heard my name.

"Hey Cesar." A racy high-pitched voice greeted as she walked right past me dressed in all black and revealing the most attractive smile.

"Hey." I answered in a silently as I was confused that they were even speaking to me.

It was something that they never did. I didn't even know they knew I existed but now that I knew it was something that I knew I was going to start paying attention to. Yolo was my man, a hundred grand, but no matter how great we got a long it was hard for me to trust him considering the line of work that we were in. He could off me at any moment while my guard was down and I'd be none the wiser. Then the Cleaners would be scraping my body off the couch. Naw, I could never be caught slipping like that. Never.

**Mink

"Thanks baby. I appreciate all my new shit today." I smiled wiggling my pretty ass out of the car with my expensive bags in tow.

"Yeah you just make sure you have that pretty ass all ready for me in the morning cause I'm coming to get that ass that I just paid $6500 for." Cash replied licking his lips.

"Yeah whatever nigga." I mumbled as I shut his door and walked on down the street.

His scary ass couldn't even take me to the front door of my apartment complex and he's demanding pussy. It wasn't like he spent heavy cash on me. I only got a few bags not a whole fleet full of shit like I wanted but nonetheless I knew he would get this pussy. Yeah, he'd get this pussy after two hours of eating it first. As I neared the complex, I noticed that everybody and their mommas where out there watching as I walked up in my new Louboutin pumps and designer bags. I loved being the envy of the scene. Hating ass people didn't bother me one bit. Just as I hit the stairs my phone vibrated in my pocket.

"Hello?"

"Bitch, what the fuck you mean you're pregnant?" Flava yelled through the phone. "Me and momma ain't about to take care of no more of your illegitimate ass kids."

"Okay first of all, you don't take care of shit and second of all why do you even care. You need to be trying to figure out why your practically married, educated ass can't seem to hold one in your belly." I snapped sick of her shit and flicking my long weave around to my back.

"What the fuck are you talking about?"

"Don't play me for a fool, Flava. You already know momma can't hold water and she told me about your three miscarriages. Ain't nobody slow."

"Mink, you are treading on thin ice bitch."

"Oh, am I? Well right now a chick is skating just fine." My shiny glossed lips popped right before laughter filled the conversation. "Thank you very much."

"Don't get it twisted like you can't get knocked down from that pedestal you standing on. You ain't got far to fall neither, especially when that nigga finally leaves your dumb ass." Flava countered.

"Stay out my fucking business, alright? He ain't going nowhere, we are just fine, and you need to worry about who your man is stickin' his dick in tonight." I cackled. "Be careful bitch it just might be me."

"You don't want your ass royally beat, Mink."

"Oh what's wrong? Dear sweet sis can't take a little friendly competition? Better watch your back bitch cause as soon as you snooze, I'm gonna ride that dick 'til it falls off, ho. It should've been me with him anyway."

"Ugh, would you get over that already. He didn't want a hoe, he wanted a woman." She barked.

"Well it looks like he's still looking for that then huh?" My laughter was so loud it nearly rattled the stairwell.

"Don't call my phone no more."

As I hung up, I started thinking about the fact that we were never really close and she always thought she was better than me. Why we even faked liking each other for this long was beyond me. All of my conversations with her always ended in an argument about one thing or the other and I was damn sick of it. The next time I wanted to hear her voice was when she was crying through the phone because I had told her I fucked that fine as nigga of hers. That and that he was leaving her for me. Who says I can't have my cake and eat it too?

I walked towards the door turning the key and entered feeling like I was sitting on a cloud. Nothing or no one could bring me down from my natural high. Not even the phone call from five minutes ago. I was about to get my hustle on tenfold and niggas' pockets were about to be broke. It was getting dark out prompting me to cut the lights on as I dropped the bags on the carpet.

"Oh shit! Cesar, you scared the shit outta me. What you doing sittin' here in the dark?" I asked clenching my chest and breathing heavily.

"Waiting on you." He replied mildly.

"Wh...Where's the truck? I didn't even see it parked outside."

"Don't worry about that. That's not your major concern." Cesar crooned walking over towards me. "So what's in the bag? Anything for me?"

"Well, I didn't really get anything for me either. It's just a few things."

"Uh, huh. Something for CJ?"

"Huh?"

"SOME-THING-FOR-CJ?" He yelled picking up my Gucci bag checking the contents inside.

"Cesar, what the fuck are you doing?"

"I'm trying to see if you went out there to spread your legs for anybody but your damn self. You got the damn nerve to call me for rent money but you couldn't ask them niggas for it?" He was beyond mad, he was livid.

"While you talking shit, who says I didn't get the money? I was just saying you out there making money with Yolo and me and your son were here struggling so I did what I had to do." I replied calmly walking to the fridge for a drink. "It ain't like you cared enough to answer your phone. I mean you wouldn't even listen to what I had to say before."

"Fuck that, Mink. You're a ho! I had no business turning a hoe into a housewife in the first place. So I don't even blame you. I blame myself. But that's all over now."

"You're right baby. It's all over. So why don't you sit down and let me suck and ride that dick like I know you like."

For some reason it was then that I decided to look around at the apartment. It was damn near bare. He had taken the floor model stereo, and the 42" TV mounted on the living room wall. He had even taken the plants, the fucking plants that were in the living room next to the couches. I looked over into the bedroom seeing that everything looked in tact there but I was sure his clothes were gone from the closet and the dresser drawers. It slowly began to piss me off that this nigga thought he was just going to walk out the door without so much as an explanation or warning.

"Uh, what the hell is goin' on here, Cesar." I asked slamming my glass bottle of apple juice down on the counter. "I mean you're gone for weeks and then you pull this shit?"

"You still don't get it do you? When I told you to

leave before and you wouldn't, you thought I was just going to brush the shit off and keep dealing with your bullshit for our son." Cesar rubbed the hairs on his chin roughly. "You crazy as hell if you think I'm gonna forgive you this time, Mink."

"Okay but what about our fucking son? Did you even consider what this was going to do to him when he comes back from my mother's house for the summer?" I asked still looking around for shit that was missing.

"That's the thing...he's coming with me."

"What? I knew you would try to pull some shit like this. What makes you think I'm just gonna allow you to take my motherfucking son?" I spat walking up to his face pointing and pushing because I knew that pissed him off.

"You ain't never with him anyway. You don't help him with his homework and you always rippin' and runnin' the streets. You think I'm about to leave him here under your ass like that? Com' on now, be real." He snapped as he pointed back.

"But he's my son, Cesar. You can't take my son." I bellowed as forced tears flowed down my golden brown cheeks.

"And I understand that. You can see him whenever you want. But I'm taking my son and that's that." He said grabbing a backpack that looked overstuffed from off the couch tossing it on his back.

"Okay...but what about me, baby. I thought it was you and me against the world. Remember?"

"Mink, it ain't been you and me for a long ass time. It's been you, me, and that dude, this dude, and another and another. I mean for real girl keep your damn legs closed!"

"Uh uh, nigga you ain't gonna disrespect me like that; take my son and my shit up outta here. Now you gonna have to give me something. Some money or something cause you losing your fucking mind."

"Render unto Cesar, bitch!" He growled displaying the most devilish looking expression on his face, scaring the shit out of me. "Besides, all of my money is going to *our* son and my new fiancé. Now deal with that. I'm out.

His new fiancée? That was definitely news to me. My loud big mouth sister didn't even mention anything about that, which means he had to have been hiding it and possibly cheating on me too. Ain't that a bitch! He was just sitting here trying to accuse me of cheating when all the time he was out here doing the same shit. My blood boiled over times ten and all I wanted to do was search and destroy whoever this bitch was.

My knees felt weak and I was sick to my stomach still wondering who the hell had taken his heart from me. *His new fiancée!!!!* He had never even proposed to me and here it is he pops up talking about marrying somebody else. I couldn't take the rejection. I couldn't handle the fact that he would no longer be supplying me with what I wanted and was giving it to somebody else. I couldn't even think about him giving my dick to some other undeserving broad. Not someone who had manipulated him into being with them; someone who had ultimately taken my paycheck from me. And I bet I knew just who it was too. When I caught that bitch she would pay the ultimate price. My breathing elevated and my head grew light. My heart started racing as I fell to my knees.

"Cesarrrrrrrr!" I screamed at the top of my lungs.

To Be Continued

STAY UP TO DATE ON THE LATEST GOING ON WITH NICETY!

FOLLOW ME:

@NICETYCOUTURE

LIKE ME ON FACEBOOK:

.com/NICETYCOUTURE

www.nicetyzone.com

DON'T FORGET TO REVIEW!

#SUPPORTBLACKAUTHORS

#TEAMNICETY

CPSIA information can be obtained at www.ICGtesting.com
Printed in the USA
LVOW04s2128101014

408315LV00008B/54/P